Nativity

Nativity

an anthology

Edited by Debz Hobbs-Wyatt and Gill James

Bridge House

British Library Cataloguing in Publication Data

A Record of this Publication is available from the British Library

ISBN 978-1-907335-76-1

This edition published 2019 by Bridge House Publishing Manchester, England

All Bridge House books are published on paper derived from sustainable resources.

Contents

Introduction 7

Bon Voyage 8
  Adrian Naylor

Born Again 21
  Dianne Stadhams

Christingle 28
  Vanessa Horn

Christmas at the Cross 33
  Maeve Murphy

Drawn by the Sea 52
  Jeanne Davies

Emmanuel 57
  Steve Wade

Entranced 65
  Margaret Bulleyment

Fathering 83
  L F Roth

Following the Star 92
  Dawn Knox

Like a Lamb 104
  Linda Flynn

Moon-mother 108
  Elizabeth Cox

New Shoes for Christmas 116
  Nicole Fitton

Roses are Red 120
　　Aqsa Mustafa

Sharing Mary 129
　　Alyson Faye

Soaring Down 136
　　Finn Clarke

Solution 140
　　Janet Howson

Telling Lies 144
　　Paula R C Readman

The Go Girl 156
　　I L Green

The Legionary 166
　　Nicolas Siregar

The Seventh Angel 176
　　Joy Mawby

The Trip To Nativity 180
　　Jim Bates

The Unknown Path 187
　　Doug King

Tick Tock 196
　　Sally Angell

What Goes Around 205
　　Allison Symes

Index of Authors 211

Introduction

"Well, I think the theme for next year had better be nativity," said Debz.

We'd just conducted a workshop to launch the 2019 Waterloo Festival Writing Competition. We'd talked about the art of the short story and about what we particularly look for at Bridge House. One of our delegates was about to go on maternity leave so there was much talk about: birth, new beginnings and, because of the time of year, the Nativity.

Many of the stories, but not all, in this collection take place at or near Christmas time. There are a couple that deal with the joys and sorrows of the annual Nativity Play. There is new birth, rebirth or a new beginning in many of them.

Again this year it was difficult to choose. There are so many skilled writers out there. There was little wrong with any of the writing we read, but in the end we went for the strongest stories and for those tales that best interpreted the theme.

There are some familiar names in this volume and also some new writers. We treasure them all.

We hope you will enjoy our selection.

Bon Voyage

Adrian Naylor

All animals are equal, but some animals are more equal than others.

George Orwell, Animal Farm

"They came, they saw, they said 'We love Lucy too!' Yes, you wouldn't believe it, but they've been here eleven months and twenty-nine days and time is nearly up; they want our answer...!"

"Why did they come?"

"Shh! Just watch."

"...Sally Mitchell: as if we needed reminding, take us back over the biggest story ever to hit planet earth."

"Okay, Geoff. Well it was exactly one year ago tomorrow, August twenty-ninth, that a bright new star suddenly appeared in our skies. That was the first most of us knew we had been contacted for the first time by an *alien species*! Little did we know our military had been picking up their mysterious signals for over six months. As they hurtled towards us at close to the speed of light, listening stations all over the world began receiving the same four-word message. Yes, you guessed it: 'We love Lucy too.'

"They were perplexed: what was it they were hearing? News leaked out – the whole world was intrigued. Could this be a reference to the globally-loved nineteen-fifties sitcom *I Love Lucy* starring Lucille Ball and Desi Arnaz?

"Meanwhile NASA began tracking an enormous energy source – bigger than a comet, bigger than some planets, Object K133-6 – or as the public came to call it 'Moon Lucy' – got larger and larger in our skies, until by

8

August twenty-ninth she dominated the heavens of the northern hemisphere."

"What's a hemisphere?"

"Half of the world. Now pay attention, this is educational."

"Governments told us not to panic but that was easier said than done! Marshall Law was imposed in many smaller countries; here in the USA saw the biggest one-day spike in gun sales for two decades. Rumours of rogue paramilitary groups were rife, and I have to say that even this reporter was a little worried, folks!

"But we needn't have been – turns out ET really is friendly! Here's the first view we had of one of the visitors – that now familiar pear-shape silhouette with the single pincer that if you'll remember became *the* must-have toy last Christmas."

"What's Christmas?"

"Shh!"

"Moon-Lucy took up orbit and this piece of nifty hardware – a modified Apache helicopter equipped with advanced communications hardware was sent to make contact. Well it wasn't as dramatic as the films would have us believe: turns out they've been studying our many languages for decades based on the huge volume of telecommunications we've been accidentally transmitting out into space. And that first communication they heard from us all those years ago, the first thing we sent that made it out of our solar-system? Yes, it was hit TV programme *I Love Lucy*. Archivists have since concluded it was actually episode three from the 1951 run called 'The Diet' where Lucy hilariously, you guessed it, goes on a diet!

"Anyway, in exchange for handing over all the episodes of *Lucy* ever made, our visitors made us a rather startling offer… But we'll pick the story back up after these words from our sponsors…"

"There's no escaping haemorrhoids... sppp."

"Why did you fast-forward: is that bit not educational?"

"No. The bits in between are just silliness."

"Oh."

"And we're back. The weather forecast for the big day tomorrow follows; and a reminder that we will have full coverage from daybreak right through to the launch. But before that, and again, just in case you've been asleep or, ahuh, out of town for the past twelve months: Sally, where did we get to?"

"Well, Geoff, we left off just before we got to the now famous offer. Our world is dying, Geoff: looking a bit old and tired, unable to support the huge population growth in the East. As the great Billy Joel said, we didn't start the fire, Geoff: we tried to fight it, but it was starting to make things difficult for the innocent rest of us.

"Seeing this, and seeing what a highly developed civilisation we were, our visitors made us an offer. They said they had technology advanced enough to transport a *whole continent* to a newer, cleaner world far away."

"Though not far in time, time being, as Einstein rightly said, a relative concept, Sally..."

"That's right, Geoff. You and your Einstein! They effectively offered to save at least part of the over-populated planet earth, possibly to a world where the rest of the human race might emigrate in the future.

"Well – I think it's fair to say there was shock, and not a little disbelief. It took a small demonstration to convince the non-believers, an unpopulated island in the South Pacific being made to vanish as these dramatic pictures show. Wow! It's still a shock seeing that island just... disappear."

"I personally was reminded of Saint 'Doubting' Thomas

being invited to place his hand in Our Lord's side, as I watched that, Sally..."

"Erm... of course you were, Geoff. As I was saying after the demonstration the debate heated-up. The visitors – the Lucians, as they were christened – gave us one year to decide which continent would be allowed the one-way-ticket to... well, to paradise.

"The UN proposed a six-month enquiry to decide. The World Health Organisation suggested quicker action, and that it would be fairest to send Africa as the poorest, neediest continent. The Middle East was thrown into chaos – no change there, Geoff – with threats including nuclear devices if you believe the internet. The EU held a week-long emergency council during which it was concluded that only nations attached to mainland Europe would be counted. Britain had a sudden, snap referendum. But then there was doubt about whether Switzerland would be allowed to go, and if not, would they be left as an island..."

"Plus, how would they get all the chocolate out."

"Thanks for that, Geoff.

"Worse was to follow: the European countries couldn't even decide on how to decide. Germany proposed a basket of hard economic indicators. France proposed a fashion-based points system. Italy suggested football whilst Great Britain claimed it should be based on wider cultural influences namely that fact they produced The Beatles and still had a Queen. The Netherlands pointed out that they also had a Queen, had far more environmentally-friendly transport and had produced Van Halen. *Billboard* magazine pointed out the Van Halen brothers relocated at a very early age and the Dutch had to fall back on Golden Earring and their hit 'Radar Love', which rather undermined their argument.

"Picking up the environmental argument there was then the unseemly 'league tables' produced over who polluted

11

the earth the most, and those very unfair and dare I say 'fake' graphs that labelled the US as the worst offender. I don't think anyone came away from that looking good.

"I think we all remember that chaos reigned for a good three months. NASA, trying to find out more about the powerful technology to be used asked if there was scope for more than one continent, or for a completely hypothetical selection or exclusion of individual countries. The Lucians said no.

"But no matter: quite unexpectedly the governments of the world got together and in fact within another six weeks had come to a unanimous decision.

"We all recall that fateful night, the results show was broadcast live to over three billion, with the winners of all six continents' *X-factor* appearing on the same fabulous stage! Though what the other six billion were doing heaven knows! And of course, we all know now that the country – sorry, *continent* – chosen to make the historic journey, pioneers for mankind as they have been throughout history, is good old North America!"

"Thanks, Sally well as you say, exciting times! Now we've been providing advice on preparations for the journey and what to expect when we all get there. To help us answer your questions tonight we have assembled an expert panel from the scientific community alongside some of your favourite reality TV stars…

"First question to the panel: what to wear for the journey…?"

"Arrr! Why are you fast forwarding? Does it get silly again?"

"Most of it's silly, but it's important we learn from this – you may not think these people have anything to do with us but it's history, our history. And if we don't learn from it…?"

"We're doomed to repeat it."

"That is correct. Now – this is the day of the launch. Settle down, class."

"Good morning America! And welcome to live coverage of what is already being termed, the 'New Independence Day'."

"Why are you switching over?"

"I want you to see another channel. That was the people who were going, this is some who weren't. It's important to get different perspectives."

"Perspectives?"

"Views, opinions – what they think. This footage is priceless: it doesn't tell us what happened – I can tell you that – it tells us what the people were actually thinking. Here..."

"Welcome back to BBC Breakfast. Well, looks like they're off then, on what some are already calling *our* 'Independence Day'. Better or worse than Brexit? You decide. Send us your thoughts. In the meantime, Carol, what's the weather going to be like for the big day?"

"So the ones left behind didn't mind?"

"Some did, some didn't. There was talk of corruption around how the decision was made. As soon as it was made there was an immediate lock-down of people entering North America: walls were built. But there were rumours of government officials from other countries – ones who'd voted for North America – sneaking in. When the dust settled there was a feeling in the rest of the world that they may just be better off without North America. The wealthier nations saw a reduction in competition; the poorer as there being one less nation to bully them. And everyone agreed that, in theory, there were less mouths to feed so more resources to go around; the Americans used more than their fair share."

"Why?"

"Just because; when you're big you tend to get to do what you want. And, of course they thought they were going to the promised land – just like when they'd first arrived on the continent many hundreds of years before."

"You said thought *they were going: did they not get there?"*

"Watch and learn, child."

"So just how is this unimaginable feat going to be achieved? Over to Lawrence Tetley, the BBC's Science Correspondent who takes up the story."

"Just how *do* you help a continent leave the Earth? That of course was the big question in the early days of the Lucerian's visit. In fact, only once they'd performed their demonstration on the island of Manuti in the South Pacific did people really start to believe it possible. But an island no bigger than Birmingham is one thing – North America is quite another. The island was removed using something called a 'graviton-field', a technique hypothesised by scientists in the sixties but never proven, at least by humans. But even they admitted it isn't powerful enough to lift an entire landmass.

"An additional complexity came with the revelation that it was not now the North American continent that was chosen to 'emigrate' but just the United States itself. Conspiracy theories abounded, but from a technical point of view this meant the country would effectively have to be 'carved-out' from Canada to the north and Mexico to the south. The recently-erected boundary wall ironically providing a helpful marker for what will soon be a new coastline.

"Here you see the first wave of tiny, self-directing robots – the so-called 'nano-diggers' – dropping from

14

Moon-Lucy to the applause of crowds. Only six-inches across each can shift ten-times its weight in earth each and every second, and as you can see there were millions deployed. Our graphic shows how they are designed to 'eat' down into the earth, creating a fifty-yard wide, mile deep channel at the border, before turning to eat right beneath the chosen land-mass before emerging at the sea.

"They performed the first successful 'separation' on Alaska last month and with only limited unplanned disruption – here we see some of the property accidentally destroyed: a town which thought it was leaving will actually now be staying, but the population have been given the option of crossing to the emigrant landmass over myriad temporary but strictly controlled bridges.

"Indeed, these new border controls have been amongst the more controversial aspects of the entire operation. With the earth in the ecological situation it is, many consider departure to a fresh, clean world a good thing. But that's by no means everybody. We've seen as many people trying to leave the United States as trying to enter. Land of the Free indeed.

"Well, the nano-diggers completed the carve-out of mainland USA last week, the last of the bridges was demolished at midnight yesterday, and now we wait with bated breath to see how the visitors are going to lift it. Lawrence Tetley; BBC Science Correspondent: Toronto."

"Thank you, Lawrence. Well of course there is still that very big question: 'How will they do it?'. And there are those who remain sceptical, convinced it may still be a con-trick.

"With us on the sofa is Irene Lethrington, Professor of Engineering at Manchester University, and Kevin Pritchard who runs the website 'Conspiracy: or is it?' Let me turn to you first, Professor…"

"Arr! We were watching that!"

15

"You can't watch all of it, it's getting late. You need to watch the important bits. See..."

"...and with the big clock behind me counting down – only... three hours to go – the crowds down here in Times Square continue to go wild! Back to the studio, Sally."

"Thank you very much, Christie; Christie will be reporting live throughout the day. Well after all the discussions and the debates, after the tests and the digging, today's the day folks, a new future for America!"

"So, they were happy to leave?"

"Very."

"And everyone else?"

"Not as happy, but maybe happy enough."

"Why?"

"Not everyone likes everyone else, you know that. We get on better with others like ourselves."

"I get on with everyone, Miss!"

"No you don't: what about the birds – you don't like birds."

"But no-one likes the birds, they're not like us..."

"There you go. Or wasps."

"Same with wasps!"

"And that's how it starts. Anyway, I've fast-forwarded to an important bit: now watch this."

"So, Kevin Pritchard: you've heard the technical evidence – it can be done. So, what's your evidence that all may not be as it seems?"

"This recording, intercepted by members of our Web Community yesterday..."

"Sorry... recording of whom?"

"The visitors – *them*. They're talking about us..."

"But even our authorities have no contact with them?"

"Yes, they do – the government have been lying: they've been listening, they know what's really going on."

"And what *is* really going on, Kevin?"

"Listen to this recording we intercepted from them!"

"…We had thought the creatures were advanced, that they were outward looking and eager to evolve. But closer examination has revealed this not to be the case. Unfortunately, the planet is infected. We have identified the cause and are about to remove it so that the planet may renew itself. The cure is drastic, but necessary…"

"Hang on, sorry but I thought they did not speak English?"

"We had to run it through a translator we found on Google…"

"Sorry this all sounds immensely far-fetched!"

"No, no – they know: *our government* know – they know that the Americans are being removed but they will all be killed! And they don't care: they and the other western governments think they'll be better off without them! It's all a conspiracy! Hey – get off me! Ow! *Get your hands off* – I know my rights…!"

"Apologies for the interruption there, viewers. Obviously, there are differing views about what's taking place. That was – ahem – one of the more extreme ones! Anyway – I see from the clock in Trafalgar Square that there is less than an hour to go now – and the crowds in London are just as excited as they are in Paris, Madrid, New York, Washington – you name it! This really is the event of a lifetime. In years to come your grandchildren will ask: where were you on Independence Day…?"

"*What was that man saying – that they weren't being taken to a better world after all?*"

"*That's what he said.*"

"*And was he right?*"

"*We have no way of knowing, do we? Not now.*"

"*Oh. So, what happened?*"

17

"Okay last part: here we are for the lift-off. Watch..."

"Welcome back and as the clock ticks down, just *look* at the vast, jubilant crowds across the US and indeed in London, Rio and Moscow where the populations have gathered to wish us all well. Look at them! Hundreds of thousands – no, millions of people, the greatest farewell in history!

"With just five minutes to go we now pass to... yes, I'm being told it is the White House; for an address by the President.

"Ladies and Gentlemen – the President of the United States."

"My fellow Americans: once more this great nation of ours stands on the precipice of history. Once more we go forth into the unknown as proud pioneers, not just for our fine nation, but for the whole human race. And this time it isn't the army, or the astronauts or the scientists who lead us there: it is all of us – every single US citizen who is at the vanguard as we seek our destiny amongst the stars. We have conquered this world; now it is time we sought a new challenge and conquered a fresh one. We take not just our spirit, our ingenuity and our resolve: we take the very soil beneath our feet. And of course, we take our souls. God bless us, God bless the Lucerians, and God bless America!"

"Well, stirring words from the President there and you can see what they meant to the crowds. Judging by the faces and body language possibly a little less well appreciated in other countries but hey: jealousy's a horrible thing, right?"

"I don't know about you, Geoff, but I'm getting just a tiny bit nervous. The clock says... yes, just one minute to go! Are you ready, folks – are you ready for the ride of your life? Have you secured your valuables?

"Thirty seconds! Hold on to someone or something tight: this may get bumpy!"

"The people in all those cities are all cheering..."

"Ten... nine..."

"They all believe things are about to get better."

"Six... five..."

"But they messed this world up..."

"Four... three..."

"All of them..."

"Two..."

"They're..."

"One..."

Pause.

"Floating! All the people are floating, Miss! How did they... the gravity thing."

"Yes."

"But... it's not just the Americans – all the other sorts, in all the other cities – they're all floating up too!"

"That's right – all of them."

"So... the Lucerians, they took all of the people instead of the land?"

"Yes: the land's still here – you're standing on it."

"But no people anymore?"

"Nope – there are no people left at all. These are the last television broadcasts ever made. After that: nothing. No radio, no internet – nothing."

"Wow! So that crazy-man was right – the aliens did mean to take the people? But not just the American ones, ALL of them. That was the 'cure' to make the planet better?"

"Looks like it."

"And did it? Did it make the planet better?"

"Well – that's rather up to the rest of the animal kingdom now, isn't it?"

"And was it them who taught us to talk?"

"Indeed they did, as a kind of leaving gift I suppose.

19

And the first thing they did was to leave us a message. It boomed out from Moon-Lucy as that bright-light revolved round the Earth one last time.

"It said 'Make sure you look after it for us better than the last lot.'"

About the author

Adrian Naylor, 49, took up writing late in life but has made up for it with a spectacular lack of success.

Three novels await publication whilst short story *Horseflesh* was included in Bridge House Publishing's 2018 Anthology *Crackers*, and novella *Four Fridges* has sold a few copies via Amazon. Family and friends have been supportively ambivalent.

Adrian is married, lives in Northumberland and is part-owned by Leffe, their cocker-spaniel.

Born Again

Dianne Stadhams

In the most famous of nativity stories donkeys, cows, sheep, wise men and a star in the east featured big time. However the men in this story were not wise. None of them were called Joseph or Jesus. The women weren't named Mary but they've all given birth. The action did not happen in stables but within walking distance of London's Bethlem Hospital, a place that changed its use from national mad house to a war museum of global status. There are allegorical animals in this story but no miracles.

As our characters have signed the Official Secrets Act there is a need to protect their identities (especially my own) so dramatic licence has been invoked and aliases assigned to the key players – Naive Neville (newbie with a lot to learn about crucifixion), Tigress Tanvi (wannabe Herod), Spineless Sam (treading water before imminent family leave), and Jobs-worth Jason (of questionable ability to manage product, process or people). The large supporting cast, some of whom were sheepish, others shone brightly from afar and all neighed, won't feature in this short hybrid version of nativity crossed with Snow White.

But the question for us all, player or reader, is survival. Do you wither under the strain of injustice or find a way to be born again and triumph?

Read on and draw your own conclusions.

Once upon a time (like very recently) Naive Neville got the job of his dreams. It was a slog to get that far. His qualifications and experience were one thing. Government vetting and security clearances were quite another. Gestation from job offer to first day in the office took nine months. Naive Neville geared up for the challenge, navigated the passage through the electronic entry system and hit the starting block in the office smiling with stamina. The fact that conditions agreed at interview were not reflected accurately in his contract that finally arrived weeks after commencing work didn't seem a big issue to the man with a new mission.

Oops... Naive Neville's first mistake... he assumed the anomaly could be fixed easily.

The work was everything Naive Neville hoped – stimulating, challenging and an introduction to a new world of information and players. However the contract variation became a problem very quickly.

'Hi Ho, Hi Ho, it's off to work we go', according to the seven dwarfs' ditty but that's not so easy when you have to juggle child care with work demands. Naive Neville's solution was to seek guidance from his line manager, Spineless Sam who, in the interests of a quiet life with a swollen belly, referred it to next level command, Tigress Tanvi.

Oops... Naive Neville's second mistake. He anticipated an outcome that would satisfy the needs of all the workers in his food chain.

However, little did he know that Tigress Tanvi had history (of the negative kind) with Spineless Sam and many of the supporting cast who mistrusted and avoided them both. Tigress Tanvi had a thing (and not in a good way) about younger members of her team who were keen to succeed. Her management style was tough tiger – treat them mean, feed them the basics whilst preening her claws whenever possible. If someone's work fell short of her demands she berated them publicly.

The result was Naive Neville got no tangible guidance from one and a sneering jibe about his single parenthood status from the other. Duly noted and chastened Naive

Neville beavered away. There were targets to meet, training courses to complete, information to gather and share plus lots and lots and lots of meetings. Official secrets might be an exciting world to be part of but it was quite unlike Naive Neville's previous experience.

"How does everyone keep up?" Naive Neville asked his line managers.

"Intra-office diary on your computer," he was told.

"It won't give me access," he reported.

Spineless Sam and Tigress Tanvi rolled their eyes.

"Government system," they said. "You're on probation. What do you expect?"

Naive Neville had no answer for that one. Nobody else did either except to advise that one day it would come to pass for him as it had for them.

"It's called civil service ç'est la vie... enough said," was the office consensus. Hi ho, Naive Neville used his initiative and got on with the job, delivering what he was asked on time and within budget. For some of the time all went well. Other times the atmosphere simmered with resentment as Tigress Tanvi roared undeserved rebukes. On one occasion she swore loudly at Naive Neville. Enough was enough, he reported her to Jobs-worth Jason... who took no effective action. Nobody was surprised at that except Naive Neville.

Oops... third mistake... and it turned Tigress Tanvi toxic. An achieving newbie who used his initiative to challenge her territory needed radical treatment. Like her namesake she was a solitary predator who specialised in camouflaged ambush, ready to pounce... unlike donkeys, sheep and cows that tend to moan loudly but bite sparingly.

The siege was short and savage. Tigress Tanvi listed his presence in the office using the electronic data from the security entry system. The intra-office diary presented no audit trail of Naive Neville at all. He was mauled, evidence was manipulated to suggest that he had defrauded his employer by being absent from the office without permission or discussion. Wounded and depressed Naive Neville resigned. His nightmare had ended.

But Tigress Tanvi wasn't satisfied. Her bloodied prey needed to be buried. She filed a gross misconduct charge, which if successful, would disqualify Naive Neville from ever working for government again. In an attempt to pervert the course of the process she appointed herself the investigating manager. The supporting cast lowered their heads, sighed silently at yet another deposed colleague and resigned themselves to the inevitable.

In the most famous nativity the Magi turn up unannounced with good tidings and gifts. In Snow White the seven munchkins saved their charge from unjust oppression and oblivion. Naive Neville wasn't a church goer or a reader of fairy tales. He resigned himself to job hunting. So when Not Dead Yet, a wise old retiree from back in the day, appeared in his life advocating strategic action he wasn't convinced that the battle to save his reputation was a starter.

"Born again?" Naive Neville grimaced. "Not in my life time!"

"Ah, you must have faith, newbie," Not Dead Yet replied, "hark the herald hocus-pocus. I will help you battle the hostile hydra."

"How do you propose to do that?" asked the disillusioned sceptic.

"Process, the power of process must not be under-valued. I will show you the way with words."

Did you know that the Ministry of Defence guidance for personnel runs to one hundred and eleven pages? No,

Naive Neville didn't either. He does now. He's read the lot and would be prepared to meet his fate on *Mastermind*.

The war of words, round one, began. Naive Neville, mentored by Not Dead Yet, successfully applied, in the name of transparency and fairness, to have Tigress Tanvi removed from the process. She couldn't be the prosecutor, judge and jury, they argued. That piqued the hissing feline but satisfied the authorities that due diligence was being observed.

A new investigation manager was appointed, the case presented with supporting evidence and the findings submitted to the decision manager – none other than Jobs-worth Jason. As he deliberated Tigress Tanvi pawed her patch and marked her territory. The supporting cast kept their heads down lest they too became fodder.

Jobs-worth Jason dodged the task by failing to read the evidence in a full and proper fashion, thereby delivering a libellous and unsafe decision that contradicted the investigation manager's recommendation that there was no major case to answer. In addition he excluded mitigating circumstances of bullying against Naive Neville by Tigress Tanvi. The supporting cast were lowing. Tigress Tanvi slept well. Not Dead Yet shook his head and advised, "Hi ho it's back to battle we go. Let the charge of the munchkins begin."

The war of words, round two, began in earnest, not with a star in the east but most definitely with a deluge of email support and witness statements from the sheep and the donkeys who were incensed by the constant burden put upon them by their bully-babe boss.

"We shouldn't have to work with a tiger," they chorused. "Tigers never change their stripes."

"Mmm," mused Not Dead Yet, "evidence suggests that's not a strictly accurate quotation but I understand your sentiments. And here's the plan."

25

"What does it involve?" Naive Neville asked. "I'm not optimistic given what's happened to date."

Not Dead Yet advised that they would lodge an appeal and request an external, impartial adjudicator who had no history with any of the cast to take charge. Tigress Tanvi and Jobs-worth Jason were miffed. But rules are rules and one hundred and eleven pages decreed the process lawful. An independent appeals manager was appointed and witness statements accepted from the supporting cast. Result!

So what happened next? Was the massacre of the innocent averted? Was anyone crucified for the management misdemeanours? Was there a resurrection of proper process?

That, dear reader, is for the next instalment when it's safe to defy the Official Secrets Act and reveal the minutiae. Watch this space and in thirty years all will be revealed!

In the interim be assured that rumour has it things are not as they were. Tigress Tanvi has been muzzled and exported to civil service Siberia for re-education. That excludes her from managing two-legged animals but ranks highly the merits of ordering toilet rolls and teabags for the supporting cast. They refer to her as Toothless Tabby and have revoked her invitation, in perpetuity, to the office Christmas party where they howl carols as the Munchkin Mangers.

Jobs-worth Jason is still just that and will likely finish his days as such with nobody offering to buy him a farewell drink on retirement... not even Spineless Sam who returned to work after six months family leave with a plan to extend her family, ad infinitum, as soon as possible.

Not Dead Yet shuffles around the bowels of the building, his eyes peeled for newbies in distress. Everyone invites him to every party as a real live insurance policy. They know they may need him in the future.

And a reliable source states Naive Neville has been born again. He's now known as Napalm St Nev, patron saint of all who pass through the electronic entry system.

About the author
Dianne Stadhams is an Australian, resident in the UK, who works globally in poverty alleviation, peace and reconciliation projects and has a PhD in communications for development. Her website www.stadhams.com gives details. She has had two plays developed with Bristol Old Vic, two novels shortlisted for global competitions and a young adult novel accepted for publication. She is writing a third novel and an illustrated volume of haiku about hats. Her latest collection of illustrated short stories, *Links*, is available through Amazon.

Christingle

Vanessa Horn

And in despair I bowed my head.
"There is no peace on earth," I said.
Henry Wadsworth Longfellow

Christmas Eve. Dots of candlelight flicker about the old church, skirting the nooks and crannies etched by pillars and crevices and sketching indiscernible shadows onto the marbled ground. Frontwards – within the aptly-named sanctuary – the vast stained-glass window shows Jesus smiling benignly amidst his humble flock. All is well; is the same as it's always been, ever since every person who comes to worship here would remember. Safe. Reassuring. Unchanged.

The heavy oak doors creak open, letting in the warmly-attired villagers one by one, clustering together and cheerfully greeting each other. Air-kissing. Hugging. Repeated phrases: "Best time of year… lovely decorations… done us proud" echo sporadically in varying tones of pitch and volume, and at the head of it all – from the pulpit – Father John stands tall and smiling, ready for this, his favourite service of the year.

When everyone is seated and the agreeable pleasantries have petered to a gentle hush, the vast organ begins puffing out the introduction to the opening carol. Now, as one, the congregation stand, turning their service booklets to the first page. *Away in a Manger.* Some sing with gusto, others less confidently; regardless, the combined effort reaches the rafters and liquefies around the cavernous space, repeating snippets of notes long after they have been first sung: a cacophony of carol.

On the second verse Father John nods and raises his hand to usher forth the small group of children who have been waiting at the back of the church. One after the other they start up the aisle, clutching their Christingle oranges and nudging each other – some in excitement, some awkwardly sensing that they are just a little too old for this. The slightly unkempt parade induces 'Awws' and 'Ahhs' from many of the congregation as they recall how they too were once part of this ritual, differing quantities of years ago.

But… as the last note of the verse rings out, it is accompanied with not a full stop but a question mark, for the final child standing in front of Father John is unknown: completely unfamiliar. To everybody. And, compared to the ever-animate faces of the other children, this boy's expression lacks energy and colour as he stares at the vicar, steely-eyed and insolent in appearance. The villagers turn to each other with eyebrows raised, unspoken questions on their lips.

Father John, appearing taken aback by the impassive confidence of this stranger but ever mindful of his duty, bends down to take the orange from the child and, as he does so, his fingers touch the boy's hand. Boom! A white-gold flash suddenly throws them apart and cloaks both man and boy, plus those in the immediate vicinity, in a haze of smoke. Then, in the confused miasma, the candles dotted around the church begin to flicker and extinguish one by one, leaving an eerie darkness punctuated only by the occasional patch of smoke. A collective intake of breath follows, elongating and swaying until the churchwarden at the back of the church fumbles to flick the main switches on, flooding the building with bright, artificial light. Blinking rapidly, the congregation turn their eyes back to the pulpit and to where the boy was standing. But neither the child nor Father John is there.

Amidst the confusion, the vicar's wife swiftly rises from her front-row seat and comes forward to the lectern. The congregation relax somewhat; she will sort out the situation, for that is what she does. Cataloguing and organising the unexpected is her undisputed role in life. Her eyes fall onto the young boy's Christingle, now discarded on the floor, and she picks it up, frowning as she does so. Unlike the malleable and juicy-looking contributions of the other children, this orange appears shrivelled and withered. Dead. As she holds it up, still without comment, the congregation murmur to themselves, anxious for the situation to be resolved. Normality is taking too long, surely? There's indecision. Wariness. Some people rise, thinking they will leave to go home, needing the warmth and reassurance of cosy armchairs and banal television more than ever before.

But as they do so, a piercing squeal penetrates the mumbled hesitancy and immediately after, all is silent again. The cry has come from one of the youngest choristers sitting at the end of the stalls. Lurching to his feet, he points wordlessly to the huge stained-glass window which dominates the front of the church. In unison, the villagers follow his gesture, also staring at the window. They blink and gasp at the representation that greets them: Jesus no longer takes pride of place in the image but, instead, has been replaced by the child – the unknown boy. He is large in image and bold in colour, and his eyes – no longer opaque and lifeless – now have deep sparks of vibrancy – an arrogance, even – within.

Too much has happened now – too much that is incomprehensible – and many of the congregation shrink back into their winter best, trying to retreat from the inexplicable. Others, those younger and less superstitious, exclaim and shake their heads: there has to be a logical reason for this strange occurrence; there must be an explanation of some sort? As they deliberate, the vicar's wife lays down the emaciated Christingle orange then sweeps her stare around the expanse of the church, concerned only for her husband: where is he; where is he?

After some moments, an unfamiliar shuffling sound edges into the questioning and speculation. Gazes gradually turn, one by one, to where the sound seems to be originating – the back of the church – watching and waiting. The noise increases in volume and, finally, Father John is seen staggering from the sacristy, his usual spring and bounce reduced to a shambling hobble. He continues until he reaches his wife and then lowers himself heavily onto a vacant pew near her, his whole body wilting. Drooping. Emotion radiates from him, bowing and sagging his whole body. Sorrow? Guilt? No-one is sure exactly, but they continue to wait and watch, watch and wait, breath held and bodies still, unsure what has happened: what *is* happening.

Finally, after what seems like a lifetime but is possibly only a few minutes, Father John raises his head. Slowly. Painfully? Now the congregation closest to him can see the tiny beads of sweat standing out on his forehead, like pinpoints on a map. The vicar raises his arm and unclenches his hand, revealing a small metal crucifix in his palm. Staring intently at this object, appearing surprised by it, he shakes his head back and forth, muttering to himself. Then he turns his gaze to his wife. After a moment of hesitation – uncertainty – she moves closer to him until, finally, she can make out the words he is muttering. She frowns, then turns to repeat them to the congregation around her, her voice wavering but clear enough to be heard. *"For hate is strong, and mocks the song of peace on earth."*

31

About the author

Vanessa Horn is a teacher from Havant, Hampshire. She began writing for adults in 2013 and has been placed in many national and international competitions. Her first collection of short stories – *Eclectic Moments* – was published in 2015, and she has a book of flash fiction with a musical theme – *Theme and Variations* – being published next year.

Vanessa ventured into writing for children three years ago, and this year won the Swanwick Children's Fiction Competition (in association with *Writing Magazine*), with another of her picture book texts – *Waaaaaaaaaaaaaaaa!* – due to be published in 2020.

Christmas at the Cross

Maeve Murphy

Early nineties

I posted the letter; into the red letter box.

There was a dusked blood shot, shell shocked sky hanging over the Saint Pancras sky line. The street was empty, an ominous silence. Then came the sound of dogs barking, viciously spilling out onto the street. A Japanese man walked out of the courtyard opposite. I walked back, up the stairwell and into my flat.

Okay it was the pits. There's no point denying it. I mean I could say it was some kind of lifestyle choice, some kind of protest. But I was lost, totally lost, that was the truth of it. Dazed, concussed, staggering like a three-legged dog trying to find its way, blinded by a dazzling razor of winter sunlight, deafened by the bleating of car horns.

I was twenty-three, alone, adrift, and living in the shite hole of Kings Cross. A spit, a wink and a toss away from the scag-heads and prossies. A free falling woman. Oh yes sexual desire had brought my downfall. Fate had knocked me. Not quite unconscious but I was spaced out, floating in cotton wool. My life set on a timer, ticking away, finally had blown up. Trapped in the debris, I couldn't get out. If I went 'home' I would end up doing what my parents wanted. I wanted to play music and be a musician. But since meeting Kieran I had stopped even doing that.

I was consumed by Kieran.

I'd been deluding myself that my increasing decreasing situation was interesting, life on the margins. And now as I sat in my shitty sleazy flat, on the torn ripped sofa with bits of yellow foam bleeding out, I was in shock. Something terrible had happened and I had posted a letter. I had referenced the attack to the attacker. But what would happen now?

My neck still hurt. It was the run up to Christmas and I hadn't posted my cards yet.

Last night I had gone to bed and left Kieran next door in the sitting room of his new flat in Liverpool. I felt a bit heady because of the joint we had smoked. He'd had coke too. I fell asleep quickly. Then a couple of hours later I was woken by Kieran pouncing on me, waking me, throttling me. I remember the shock. A feeling of raw fear spreading rapidly. Inner panic.

"No," I said, trying to stay calm. He was in a dream and would wake up.

"Yes," he said.

It was that 'yes' that was terrifying. It was cool, deliberate and conscious. His quiet Liverpool accent sounded threatening for the first time. I tried to push him off but he was a big man. It was impossible. Unstoppable.

"Stop it, please you're hurting me!" I couldn't breathe. The air was getting darker. My head was getting lighter. He let go.

I walked into the toilet, shaking. Was it because in the pub, I persuaded him not to get involved in a fight? Kieran had a glass in his hand, ready to smash it. I told him the police would be called. Had I made him, the tough guy, run away from a fight? Was he in rage over that? Adrenalised from that? My fault then. I'd stopped him. But why?

In the loo I heard the sound of the front door being locked. My head whirled. I could stay in there but I thought I would attempt normality, so I went back in to the bedroom and he instructed me to give him a blow job. Terrified I complied.

I must have then slept. He must have been there. All I

remember is this morning waking up and feeling very calm, almost at peace, kind of floating. He was lying beside me, but I had my back to him. I remember feeling this very tender kiss on my back. I didn't respond, just lay there, not wanting to speak. Kieran got up and made me breakfast, something he had never done before. A fry of sausages and bacon and eggs.

In my cotton wool world I had breakfast with him. Then he walked me to the train station. The last thing he said it me yesterday was, "It'll harden you."

It was absolutely chilling. A full admission. No remorse. Yes, he was saying, he'd ground my face in the mud, stamped on it and somehow that was a good thing. He was the boss.

Only three months before I had been living in a beauty of a flat in Camden town. Spacious, with wooden beam floors and white walls. Camden has a wonderful way of tying everything together with a bonhomie boho bow. I was having a good time, being young, not thinking about much else. I was so caught up with Kieran and his showbiz friends. It was exciting, like being around them made me really successful as well. Sex and coke and late night Soho.

I didn't notice that my flat mate had missed her last three rent cheques. I couldn't afford to pay her rent as well or the deposit for another flat. Rory, a guy I vaguely knew from a late night Greek restaurant in Chalk Farm, was going travelling for a year. As long as the Housing Association didn't find out, I could stay in his flat, up four flights of stairs in a condemned red brick Victorian East End dwelling called Mid Hope House.

Having now posted the letter and back inside, I sat in fog-filled shock, chain smoking on the ripped sofa and staring

35

into space. I shouldn't have sent it. I felt like the walls were slanting, narrowing, tilting across, closing in on me.

The phone rang. I jumped. A college friend Ava. I tried to tell her what had happened. She said something about weird things can happen in relationships. *Really?* I finished the call. Ava had a new job, was getting married, she was busy. Too busy.

I still hadn't cried.

I got up. Night had fallen. I don't know how many hours had passed. The Italians were whistling their drug-selling code to each other outside. I never quite worked it out: if it was to warn each other if cops were about, or whether it was to let them know of some more stuff. They had their mad wee rituals anyway – people nodding to other people and then some runner stuffing the gear somewhere for the pick-up. The black guys did the crack, they kind of opted for the deft hand to mouth, or hand to anus technique. To be honest when I first moved in, I always thought those guys, with their hooded tops, standing in packs near York Way, looked like they were acting the hard men in some New York film. But that rose-tinted thought quickly evaporated when I saw some beat the shit out of a guy in an alley. They weren't acting, they were just really fucking mean.

I got up and looked out the window.

Opposite down below, just outside the entrance of the other Housing Association come squat was a very tall thin Asian woman, leaning against the wall, smoking a cigarette, half lit by a street lamp. I stared. There we were… I sat back down on the sofa.

There was a knock on the door. My heart rate turned up a notch. Through the weird fish eye lens I saw it was the prostitute that had been on the street, under the street lamp. I opened the door a tiny bit.

"What is it?" She had such an intense presence, penetrating staring eyes. Nothing about her was trying to please, but there was a kind of tenderness about her. She had black bags under her eyes, stood thin in her lycra black mini dress. She was beautiful, her features were delicate but her skin was rough. London Asian, that was unusual for a prostitute.

"Can you spare a couple of quid?"

So here I was Lady Muck, literally. But it made me feel good to feel kind of superior in my compassion. I felt for her. I wasn't her. I went into the sitting room and took out a few quid that I didn't have and handed them to her. She looked at me. Her brown eyes had a depth. The weird thing about Kings Cross is that the people who lived there, never made eye contact with the prostitutes and they never made eye contact with us.

"All I have," I replied.

I was different from her. I was not in her dreadful situation.

"Cheers." She replied in a lazy London drawl. Was I different from her?

I watched her shuffling out of the stairwell and down the road, passing a guy walking his bike in. Yesterday I was. Today I wasn't so sure.

The guy looked up and saw me with my face up against the window. I quickly moved away.

The next day I woke up hungry, tired, still scared. My dole cheque had not arrived, no money, other than shrapnel. Enough maybe for some fags and some Marathons which were cheap and filling. All I could think about was food. I rubbed my legs with my hands, because they felt so cold. A woman was going hysterical, screaming outside and someone screamed at her to shut up. I lifted the bit of cloth over the window and peeked out. It was that girl who had knocked on my door.

Poverty I tell you is the most soul-destroying thing. You spend your whole time thinking about what you can't have, and seeing as basically as money and beauty are the only two things most people seem to value, then you are the lowest of the low if you don't have either, an invisible. I would say both a skewed romantic type socialism and maybe some eastern mystics got it terribly wrong. There is nothing praiseworthy in poverty. It tightens your life to a point of rigidity and decisions are made from that cramped tense state of mind and often not wise ones. The police had by now arrived and finished talking to that girl and let her go. Her pimp or whoever the track suit guy was, stayed on talking to the police. I lowered the cloth on the window and got dressed.

I managed to speak to my sister on the phone.

"…why don't you talk to a priest?"

"A priest?"

That was kind of a weird thought. I wasn't sure about that.

I went out. I walked to the grey stone church at the bottom of Cromer Street. I was always trying to be a good person. I felt permanently at fault and always the one to blame. In Lady Muck mode I felt I should do my bit to help the poor down and outs of Kings Cross. I also had like a pain in my stomach which I ignored.

I walked down the stone steps and through the iron gates of the basement of the church which lead to the kitchen. I entered the main room. I looked at the mostly old men, battered by life. Fallen through the cracks. A lot of them were Irish, sitting around the tables, having charity soup and sandwich. I felt their silent shame. I looked at the red tinsel Christmas decorations hanging on the wall. There was a small wooden Nativity scene on the side. The figures of Mary and Joseph in the stable with the little baby Jesus in the crib with bits of artificial straw. Beside them were the Magi, the figures of the three wise kings bearing gifts. And some wooden sheep. I wasn't going home for Christmas, neither was anyone here.

I went up to the counter which was a few enamel tables put together.

"Do you need any volunteers, to help serve food? Over Christmas?"

The guy at the counter glanced at me. He held out the plate of sandwiches.

"Would you like some soup with it?"

"I was offering to help," I said mortified. I also recognised him as the guy walking his bike from last night.

He kind of smiled and looked vaguely apologetic but continued to offer me the sandwich and soup. With burning cheeks, I turned on my heel and left the building.

As I crossed the road, a tramp on his way in to get some food spontaneously hugged me. There I was in the middle of Kings Cross, being hugged by a tramp and at it made me strangely happy. Maybe I was like St Francis of Assisi.

I carried on walking and went 'home'. I sat on the pathetic ripped brown corduroy sofa with bits of yellow sponge coming out. I had planned to cover the sofa with a table cloth. But I sat instead staring at the window, not enough energy. I could sort this out myself. I just needed some session work. Or write some songs to sell.

I chain smoked about ten cigarettes in half an hour. I counted all my small change, ten pence, five pence and copper and scraped enough for another box of ten.

I walked down the several flights of stairs, bought my fags in the Asian supermarket on Cromer and was heading back when I walked straight into the guy who had offered

39

me the soup and a sandwich. I tried to pretend I didn't see him.

"I offer everyone who comes in a free sandwich!"

I turned and laughed. No point being uppity. I noticed the warmth of his brown eyes. They were lovely. There was a sparkle of wit in them. I liked his husky London accent.

"Do you work at the church every day?"

"Only occasionally."

"Do you live round here?"

"Yeah I'm flat minding for someone... I'm on Midhope."

"I live there too."

"Really?"

My jaw nearly dropped.

"Yes. On the ground floor."

I was amazed. Someone like him lived so near.

"I'm on the fifth floor," I said.

We both laughed.

"I'm just going back there."

"Me too. What's your name?" We walked together.

"David. Yours?"

"Blathnaid," I replied. "Bla, like blah blah and nid, like lid."

"Lovely... what does it mean?"

"Little flower"

We both laughed. I don't know why it was funny. It just kind of was. Maybe it was a funny place to be a little flower.

"Did you know two people were found dead of an overdose a couple of days ago in Tankerton".

That was the next building over. I shook my head.

"Did you hear?" I said, doing a Belfast accent in a gossipy way.

He laughed.

"No, I didn't know that, not my thing: heroin."

We carried on walking. I had this strange urge to hold his hand. He asked me what I was up to. I told him I was a musician but I was thinking of writing a play. A musical. About Hiroshima. He glanced at me, to see if I was serious, and judging that I was suggested I talk to Yoichi who lived in the second court yard across. His mother had survived the Hiroshima attack as a young woman.

"Really?"

He laughed. I asked him what he did, when he wasn't doing the homeless food thing. He told me that he took photographs and that occasionally they showed in national newspapers, but he was finding it hard to earn a living. I nodded. Like me.

David felt like a log in the middle of a crazy sea. And he was reminding that there was dry land, a shore...

David and I reached the place where we lived. He headed towards his flat.

"I'll drop Yoichi's phone number through your door."

I nodded. Even in my dazed state I clocked that gorgeous smile that broke David's serious face wide open. It was nice to know he was close. I plodded back up the stairs. I became aware again of this pain in my stomach. I ignored it.

I got in and lay in the bath. Unable to move. Motionless.

A knock on the door. It was dark now.

"Blathnaid, are you in there?" Kieran's voice.

I didn't move. I didn't breathe. The knock continued.

I tried not to move, but I was still shaking. I held my breath.

"I got your letter this morning. Came down on the train... open up, love."

For a split second I wanted to open the door. The way he said 'love' was tender. Loving even. Familiar. Maybe this could all be okay. I didn't open the door. I lay in the bath trembling. Finally I heard his steps as he moved away and walked down the stairwell. I heard him stop and then continue.

I got up out of the bath and wrapped a towel around me. I went to the window. I could see him walking away down the street. Relief.

The phone rang. I picked it up.

"Hello?"

There was a pause. And then the line went dead. I knew it was Kieran.

I would go to the police tomorrow. Now I would go to bed, not think about it. I didn't care if that was not what the thing the Northern Irish Catholics do. I just didn't care.

I then took a heavy wooden chair and placed it on top of another chair against the door. That didn't feel enough, so I took the really nice wicker basket which had all my shoes and placed it on top of the chairs against the door.

The phone rang again. The phone kept ringing. I didn't touch it.

Then it stopped. There was silence. Beautiful silence.

I could finally sink into the silence and sleep.

I woke up the next day and my dole cheque had arrived. I felt such joy. I had control back in my life. I walked down to the post office just opposite Kings Cross Station and cashed it, posted my Christmas cards and bought some chocolate hobnobs as a kind of treat.

A horrible energy clung to me as I headed home. Crossing the road I walked back down the narrow back streets to Hillview, into a courtyard near mine and up the stairs and along a balcony. I knocked on a freshly painted door. A Japanese guy opened it, David had slipped his mate's Yoichi's number underneath my door. He looked younger than I thought he would be, early forties, shiny kind of joyful very clear eyes. I walked in and saw a modest flat, in good nick, sparsely but nicely decorated. Carpet on the floor, a TV and a big brown wooden box or casket with brass knob handles on a small table. I was intrigued by the wooden box, my eyes drawn to it. It felt religious. I wondered if I was taking my sisters advice after all and going to see a priest.

Yoichi asked me if I would like a cup of tea or coffee. I asked if he had a green tea. He said he only had PG tips. I explained I was interested in doing a play about Hiroshima. He asked why? I said I was very interested in survivor's stories. It might be musical as I was a musician, so kind of like Noh theatre. I said it would probably need Japanese actors and musicians; it wouldn't be like Mickey Rooney in *Breakfast at Tiffany's*. Yoichi laughed, he thought this was hilarious.

He told me about his mum's experience, about how the Hiroshima bomb had happened in an instant. Everyone was just going about their ordinary lives with no expectation of it. How there was a flash of light. About how his mum said there were dead people lying everywhere. And how everything was covered in black ash. People were lying side by side inside public buildings. He said there were maggots coming out of the living who were not yet dead and they were in great pain. As soon as the maggots appeared people knew they were probably going to die. His mother did suffer radiation sickness, was in hospital, very weak and she kept fainting. He said many people committed suicide and his mum said she was tempted but she thought about her family.

"Yes," I said, jotting down a few notes into a notepad. I could hear a tune in my head.

"Does your mum feel bitter about her experience, her karma? Her like punishment."

43

Yoichi laughed.

"You believe people terrible 'sinner' who deserves punishment?"

I didn't know how to reply.

"I believe in the law of cause and effect. That's karma. So for example if you don't respect your life. And you keep making those causes to not respect your life, then your life will not be respected."

This was intellectually interesting, way better than a priest. Yoichi was looking at my neck. I hid my neck with my hand. I knew there were bruises. I had seen them.

"So it is people's fault what happens to them?"

He picked up one of my chocolate hobnobs and took a bite.

"People who hurt someone else are accountable for their actions."

I nodded.

"How does your mum feel about the pilot who dropped that bomb?"

"She's not attached to him. My mum knows her karma is her karma and the bomber's karma is his karma. She has to deal with her karma and he has to deal with his karma. If he wishes. Separate."

I found this fascinating.

"My mother now make her karma her mission."

I felt woozy.

"Mission?" That word made me think of the missions in Africa, the black babies etc.

"So she doesn't want to just kill him?"

"No. She work for peace."

I switched off. "Your mum's a saint... not everyone can be as good as that."

Yoichi chuckled. I got up and glanced at the wooden box. He watched me.

"I'm a Catholic," I said.

"Better speak to a priest then." His clear almond eyes were dancing, teasing me.

"Maybe I will."

"Drop the self-pity," he said staring at me.

I wanted at that moment to smash his happy shiny face. What a bastard! At least a Catholic priest would hear your sins and give you absolution. I didn't want to hear his heartless eastern clap trap any more. I sprung to my feet.

"Well, Yoichi, I better go. Better conversation than you normally get in confession, that's all I can say."

"Three Our Father and Two Hail Mary!" he replied.

As I walked down the stairwell, I became aware again of the pain. I touched my hand on my lower abdomen. It felt bloated, hard. I'd take some more pain killers when I got in. That's what I was thinking about as I turned the corner. Did I have enough? Should I go the shops? No – there were enough—

And there he was.

At the top of the stairs to my floor.

He was standing outside my door.

And he had seen me.

I wasn't sure whether to turn and run or to keep walking. Kieran looked at me. He didn't look angry. He looked normal. He smiled, like he was pleased to see me. What was really attractive when we first met was he really saw me, asked me questions about me, though never actually came to see me play – up until recently I had been doing small pub gigs. I noticed he looked his age, forty, normally I never thought about that much.

"I called round yesterday."

I nodded. Didn't make any comment.

He waited for me to open the door. I didn't.

45

"I've just remembered I've got an appointment at the doctor," I said.

"Are you okay?" His eyes were piercing, though his manner was friendly.

"Yes, I think so."

"Look where you're living. Jesus, Blathnaid. I got your letter... So what actually happened?"

I looked at him, gobsmacked not knowing what to say. *He didn't remember? Really?*

"I just know something terrible happened."

He looked sincere. "What happened?"

"You..."

Finding it hard to say more words, I pointed to my bruised neck. He looked away, looked disturbed.

"I'm sorry." He sounded sincere.

But was he? He said it would 'harden' me.

Maybe I did need to speak to a priest. Focus on forgiving?

"It's my birthday," he said.

"Today?"

"I'm meeting people for drinks up in the pub tonight, if you want to come up later?"

I paused. He was brushing this all off like it was nothing. He said he would see me later. I nodded. He kissed me. It was just like a normal kiss.

"I love you," he whispered. He had never actually said that before.

Maybe love could conquer all. He had just lost it, though I still didn't know why, but everyone deserves a second chance. *Don't they?*

I walked through the pub door a few hours later. He was sitting at a table with a couple of other people. They were Channel 4 documentary people who were hanging out in

46

the London Irish scene which was Kieran's thing. It was exciting to be so near these people. It made me feel like I wasn't just on the dole, I was part of it. Maybe I could do some incidental music for it. If I could pluck up the nerve to discuss that with them. I also had to be careful, Kieran sometimes got jealous. Kieran looked nice in his denim shirt. I wore a black polo neck top. There was a large real Christmas tree nearby and a show band on the stage. It was packed. People were up in festive spirit, dancing away to country and western cover songs.

"Have you brought me a blow-up doll for me birthday?" Kieran asked.

It was such a gross thing to say on so many levels, it should have sent me out the door.

Kieran then talked about me going to spend time with him again in Liverpool. I couldn't understand all these conflicting things, so I went to the ladies and re-applied my lipstick. I needed time to think.

On my way back came I heard Kieran talking to one of the guys. They had their backs to me.

"I hope you didn't mind Blathnaid joining us. I want to have a sweet night tonight. Know what I mean? Butter her up."

A throaty male chuckle erupted between them all.

My cheeks burned. Something snapped. All the stuff I'd kept hidden away from myself was now erupting. Running, backwards, forwards, round my brain.

There is a truth.

Don't say too much.

I will! I'LL SCREAM!

I picked up my red wine; threw it over him. I had such rage the glass shattered in my hands and now there was glass all over the floor, and everyone looking at me. That's when I saw the blood; dripping from my hand, red blood and soon it had become a red hand. I felt sweat on my face.

a heavy pain pulsing. He jumped out of his seat and came forward to console me, to calm me down.

"GET AWAY FROM ME!" I roared. "DON'T YOU COME NEAR ME! OR I'LL PHONE THE POLICE!"

Next thing I was pushing open the door. And then I was running.

It was raining. I was bawling. Like a junkie I'd gone back to what had hurt me – like an old habit. I hated myself. I couldn't be stronger. I couldn't make better choices. I couldn't change, so my life would never change. I was stuck like this. Stuffed. I screamed. It ripped the air. I didn't want to be a victim. I didn't want this.

The rest is a daze. I remember sitting in the tube carriage, blood streaming out of my hand. A guy further down had blood all over his white shirt. He was sitting upright, looking straight ahead as if he was fine.

I got out of the tube at Kings Cross. There were a group of people singing carols and collecting money in buckets for the homeless. Traffic on the Euston Road was buzzing past. I stepped out into the road.

That's when a hand reached out and grabbed me back as a huge lorry drove past. I looked round to see Yoichi's face. He looked furious. I was stunned. How the hell was he there? Was he like monkey from that Japanese TV series? He snatched me across the road, into the Burger King opposite just beside the post office which was alive with all the usual illicit late night stuff. Just as we entered I saw the Asian prostitute I'd lent a couple of quid to. She was there shivering with the rest of them.

Next thing I know the young African girl behind the counter was cleaning my hand with ice and then wrapping it in kitchen roll.

The face of the Asian prostitute loomed before me, looking concerned.

"Is she okay?" she asked Yoichi. "I know her."

"What's your name?" I asked.

"Nadina," she replied. "What's yours?"

"Blathnaid," I replied. "It means little flower."

We all laughed until Nadina's pimp appeared with horrible dead darting eyes, wanting to know what was going on.

Yoichi then briskly walked me out and back in the direction of my flat.

When we reached Midhope Street, we passed David returning from a night out. He looked at me.

"You okay?"

"Fuck off!"

I didn't want him to see me like this. I could see the shock in his eyes. His eyes. His beautiful warm lovely eyes. I felt like crying, all I wanted to do was talk to him. See him. Speak with him. Find out about him. Everything about him. David quickly opened his flat and went in.

Yoichi and I got up the stairs to my flat. The pain in my abdomen was now unbearable. It was coming in waves. I was bent over holding it with my bleeding hand.

I got out my key and opened the flat door. Yoichi was still with me.

"Want a cup of tea?"

Yoichi was looking at me strangely. I went into the narrow kitchen to make it.

"Blathnaid," he said quietly but in an alarmed way. He looked at my legs.

I looked down. Blood. Clumps, black clotted. A pounding in my ears. That is when I collapsed. All I remember was an ambulance man arriving and I was half carried out and down the stairs by him and Yoichi. I passed Mike the Junkie who lived below and was standing at his door with his pink shaded glasses and holding his scrawny black cat.

"Has she OD-ed?"

The guy from New Zealand who was an artist who lived opposite Mike, opened and then quickly shut his door when he saw what was going on.

We got to the bottom of the stairs. All I could think about was David but his door did not open. I'd just told him to fuck off. I really was a stupid bitch.

I was put on a stretcher. I heard the hushed word 'miscarriage'. I had missed a period. Oh my God. The ambulance driver asked me if Yoichi was my next of kin.

"I'm a neighbour," said Yoichi.

"Is there a next of kin, we need a number and address?"

"No next of kin, no room at the Inn... No Virgin birth." I mumbled delirious.

David's face and eyes loomed in front of mine. He *was* there. His eyes were so warm but he looked scared. So was I. *A baby? I was really losing a baby?*

"Come over for a bite when you get back."

"Christmas pity party?"

He took my hand and squeezed it really tightly.

They lifted me into the ambulance. I could see the tiny little narrow alley to the side, a half-eaten hamburger and a used condom lay on the ground. I suddenly saw it all so clearly. This was hell – I had to get out.

The ambulance drove off. Blue light swirling into the darkness. Another Kings Cross casualty. I swore to my life as we raced through the back streets, I would change.

'Ave Maria' was playing in my head.

It was practically Christmas Eve.

Maiden hear a maiden's sorrow,

Mother hear a suppliant child...

I could still feel David's heart in my hand. I held on tightly to that.

About the author

Maeve Murphy is an award-winning writer-director from Belfast. She studied English at Cambridge. Her first feature, *Silent Grace*, was critically acclaimed and chosen as the UK entry for Cannes and nominated for 'The Conflict and Resolution Award' at the Hamptons International Film Festival USA. It was released in the cinema in the UK and Ireland. Her second feature, *Beyond the Fire*, was selected for 'New British Cinema' at the ICA and screened on BBC 2 after encountering press controversy in Ireland due to the subject matter. It was the winner of 'Best UK Feature' at the London Independent Film Festival and won "Best International Film" at the Garden State Film Festival USA. Her third feature, *Taking Stock*, a fun film festival award-winning comedy caper, starring Kelly Brook was released in UK cinemas and 'Popular on Netflix'. It was based on her short film *Sushi* which won the Sub-ti International Film Award at the Venice Film Festival. Maeve has had articles published in the Irish Times, Mail on Sunday, and Sunday Times. She is currently writing a screenplay, a love story about Shane Mac Gowan and his long term love Victoria Mary Clarke. Maeve is co-writing this with Victoria Mary Clarke. Maeve will direct.

www.maevemurphy.net

Drawn by the Sea

Jeanne Davies

The cold metal of the wrought-iron railings imprinted hard into her back; she'd gazed for hours at the festoon of floral drapes which swamped the small wooden cross. She was reliving the final passage of the flag-draped casket as it was shouldered by stiff, awkward-walking military men. The bugles still resonated in her head, *Johnny has gone for a soldier*, as the earth engulfed the coffin.

Annie knew he wasn't here among the ancient stones encrusted with creeping yellow and brown lichen; nor was he amongst the pristine white marble standing patiently in rows. Embracing the remembrance monument with its faded ring of poppies, she hurried through the gate and fled into the street. Resisting frenzied tears, she headed towards the coast, feeling sure Johnny's spirit awaited her there with other victims of the cruel, heartless sea and its unforgiving nature.

Joining the chaos of Worthing seafront, she slipped in amongst joggers, cyclists, dog walkers, kids on scooters, and the toy train which was being bombarded by squabbling seagulls. The beach fronts of Sussex were laden with families enjoying a typical British summer with ice creams, penny arcades and all the fun of the fair, amid the underscents of greasy sun lotion. Excited children grasped onto colourful new buckets, waiting patiently as their fathers hammered windbreaks into moist recently exposed sand. All along this coastal stretch the heady smell of donuts and fish and chips blended with the undertones of the salty sea air. Annie suddenly felt nauseous.

With her long blonde hair wilting around her hunched shoulders, she walked onto the Victorian pier where Johnny and she had enjoyed their first date all those years ago. Since she was a child she'd never been drawn towards the ocean and hated the gaps between the wooden slats of the pier; but Johnny said he trusted the sea like a mother and that she should too. Often, they'd sit there on a bench holding hands to watch the fishermen, with their rugged jovial faces, haul in their catch. Tears blurred her vision as she wandered bewildered and alone with her heart dangling heavily in her chest. Snippets of conversations buzzed past her ears as people passed by wearing smells from laboratories, chatting on phones, chastising children or calling to their dogs. She did not see the frilly petticoats of tiny waves as they trickled gently towards shore; nor did she see the beauty of the twinkling ocean. She was a damaged soul, tethered and imprisoned by her grief.

Annie arrived at the busy Sea Lane café, catching sight of her pale haunted features reflected in the windows like a ghost. After many windswept walks they'd often stop here to watch the ocean and to make plans. He would give up the Navy soon he'd promised her; they'd buy a small boat where he could give sailing lessons and teach their young a true love of the ocean. Johnny was convinced they'd have big strong sons with broad shoulders like him. She walked on, wrestling with memories and unfulfilled dreams... all the life that the war had robbed them of.

Oblivious to the passing hours, she hadn't seen the beautiful crimson sunset or been aware of people slowly deserting the beach. At the end of the promenade Annie sunk down onto the shingle to gaze out across the vast sparkling ocean and the distant horizon. The sepia shadows of several vessels hung in limbo on the faded boundary between sea and sky, motionless unless she glanced away. The ocean changed its shape in a perpetual motion of dips and swells beneath the now sombre twilight sky. Dusk began to gather around her in a cloak, but she felt no urge to leave; there was nowhere she wanted to go.

She listened to the gentle 'so' of waves being sucked down, and 'ha' as they rushed back in, soothing her into a dreamlike state. Johnny's voice was calling out to her, telling her to trust the sea like a mother and join him there. Rising clumsily to her feet and stumbling towards the water, she muttered his name in whispers that were immediately snatched by the breeze. Tumbling waves now clawed at pebbles and grabbed at shells as the tide began its alluring retreat, grabbing sparkling dust down beneath each wave. The ghostly ships on the horizon beckoned persuasively to her through the canopy of the starlit sky, urging her to enter and join her sweetheart there.

She kicked off her shoes, allowing the water to lick her toes as she slowly sank into the sand in obedience to the demanding draw of the tide. She could hear Johnny's voice still calling out to her and feel his presence in the wind. Spontaneously her body launched forwards as she shouted his name into the surf which struck her brutally in the face and gurgled down her throat like liquid sandpaper. She spewed the water out and choked as the current carried her swiftly away, the swell buffeting her towards the horizon.

Annie allowed herself to drift, the waves rocking her limp body like a jellyfish on top of the water. She felt no fear; the intoxicating smell of salt reminded her of his blonde hair and coarse weathered skin. She wanted to be taken… to be sunk with Johnny's ship. She realised that she couldn't blame the sea for taking him – it was the chaos and destruction of war and the senseless weapons of man that had robbed her of him. Wherever he was… be it dark or endless night… it was where she wanted to be. She voyaged on, exposed to the elements around her and trusting that she was travelling closer to where he would be waiting for her.

As the sky blackened into the ink blackness of the sea, white crests rose to play in the moonlight. Annie permitted the darkness to wrap itself around her, feeling the rise and fall of her body rocking in the swell until sleep overwhelmed her. She slept deeply; deeper than she could ever remember. She dreamt of journeys he had told her about, the wonderful places the sea had shown to him and where he'd sent her love letters from.

Something suddenly disturbed her slumbers and stirred her senses to consciousness; a queer feeling that demanded she wake up. The sky had begun to lighten but the shoreline had completely vanished. Twisting and turning in the freezing water, she could find no trace of the bottom. Icy fingers began spreading around her body like a blanket; she struggled but was unable to move from her morgue like cocoon.

Then a giant swell rose up from behind her, a wave as high as the ship that had carried Johnny away that day to the battle zone. She stared up in wonder at the tip of the surge as it bent over her floating body like a doting mother embracing her child. Taking almost human form, it cradled and nursed her, sweeping her gently but firmly. She closed her eyes in submission. The wave picked up speed dramatically like a powerful fairground rollercoaster until, like a woman giving birth, it ejected her onto the beach.

The warmth of the early morning sun on her face persuaded Annie to open her eyes. She found herself lying like a stranded crab with arms and legs splayed out on the wet sand. She blearily gazed up at the dawn's magic writing across the sky. Two white gulls circled above her limp body, squawking plaintively to each other. Unable to move, she lay there for some while, listening to the gentle lullaby of the ocean. The sea had rocked her, soothed her and had licked all her wounds.

Eventually, Annie heaved herself to sitting, finding herself right beside the old pier. She realised she had ended her journey here, where it had all begun. When the quickening came it took her breath away... just for a second... and then it was gone; but she felt her body was glowing. She could feel the new life moving inside her... the special gift of motherhood.

As Annie struggled to climb the mountain of pebbles to the promenade; she gazed back for one last time before turning away from the cruel sea. A smile played upon her lips as her secret was confirmed now; a new beginning, a new life. How she hoped their baby would have Johnny's soft blue eyes.

About the author
Jeanne Davies' short stories have been included in several anthologies produced by Bridge House Publishing, including *Baubles, Snowflakes* and *Something Hidden*. This year her story *Everything has Changed* was selected for the Waterloo Festival anthology. Other successes include several stories published by Centum Press in the USA, *Waverley Road* by Graffiti Magazine, several flash fiction pieces published by Early Works Press in their *Sharp as Lemons* and *The Ball of the Future* anthologies. *Stagnight* was also the winner of the Earlyworks Flash Fiction competition, Jeanne had several pieces of poetry about animals published in the *Words for Wadars* anthology and was recently shortlisted by FWS Vernal Equinox as well as making the Ink Tears longlist.

Emmanuel

Steve Wade

He appeared in Ward 15 of the capital's busiest hospital on Christmas Eve. There seemed to be no record of him being admitted, but there he was lying in what had earlier become a vacant bed. A young man with a light beard and bandaged hands and feet.

Every effort to find out when he had arrived, who had admitted him, if someone had brought him in, and even who his nearest contact might be resulted in further confusion. And, on examination, they found that beneath the bandages the patient had wounds and bleeding consistent with accidental or inflicted injuries. Self-harm maybe. But, apart from feeling professionally bound to treat him, it was, after all, the season of good will, wasn't it?

A change of shift brought new staff with the same questions. One particular nurse, a foreign national, was especially taken by his charms.

"You remind me of someone," she said. "Only I don't know who." She laughed at her own comment.

"I'm just a man," he said. "Like a million other men." But his dark eyes betrayed him, as though she too might have been someone he had known but could not place.

She tried to find out more about him. To some of her enquiries he responded. He told her he was a carpenter. This tallied with his weather-beaten appearance and muscular frame. To other enquiries he either looked at her blankly or stared in the direction of the window and commented upon the now swirling snow in the darkening sky. So she tried a different approach.

"By the way, I'm Miryam," she said.

She watched his tormented yet somehow kind eyes slide

57

down her body and clamber back to her face. He smiled slightly, nodded, but didn't offer his own name. Instead he asked her about the due date of the baby she was carrying. She told him any day now, and that sure she was in the right place if her child decided to make an early entrance.

He smiled.

"So what do they call you?" she said.

Instead of replying, he lifted his hands from his lap, twisting them over as though he were examining the wounds for the first time. She told him not to worry, and that she'd have him cleaned up in a jiffy.

And so, with a basin of water and a sponge, she took in her hands the young man's right hand. But, on touching his flesh to her flesh, there shot through her a bolt of electricity. And drawn to his dark brown eyes, something invisible, divine perhaps, clutched her by the throat and left her breathless.

Unable to speak audibly, she heard in her head the words she wanted to put to him. *Who are you?* And as though he had heard her unspoken words, she thought she heard the bearded young man's voice cryptically answer *I am who I am.*

"Who did this to you?" Miryam said, finding again her voice. She frowned as she ran her fingertips across the wounds in his hands.

"It's nothing," he said, turning his mouth down while still looking at his hands. He thanked her and said that the old man opposite seemed more in need of help than he did.

The nurse twisted about, shocked to see Mr Klaus, the elderly patient in a seated position, and looking all around him. Her shock was twofold. With his family's consent, the old man had been put into an induced coma two days before. On December twenty-first, the shortest day of the year and the longest night – the Winter Solstice. A coma from which he wasn't expected to emerge, as the family had also agreed to the withdrawal of the drugs that were keeping him alive. And now, apart from being awake, he appeared to be in the peak of health for his age. His big jolly face crowded with good-fellowship. His cheeks fire-engine red. And all framed by a head of white curly hair and a full white beard.

Thirsty, the old man told her when she rushed across to his bedside. He was bursting with the thirst is how he put it.

Despite her professionalism, the nurse could have wept to hear again the quirkiness of Mr Klaus's terminology. Because, even though she would never admit to it, she and the rest of the staff had their favourite patients from time to time.

From his bedside locker, she took and uncapped a bottle of water, poured some into a paper cup and raised it to the old man's lips. With his hands wrapped about hers as she held the cup, she ensured he took it in gentle sips. The warmth of his hands a further surprise.

When she turned back to the younger man, so fast asleep was he, he might have been the one now in a coma. She then told the old man she'd be back, and off she went to the nurse's station to tell her colleagues what had just happened.

Before going back to their duties, the three nurses made surreptitious visits to the bed where the old man sat up smiling at everyone. To witness with their own eyes this man who may not have escaped his date with Death, but for now had stood him up.

The unexpected excitement and drama was overridden by the deteriorating weather. Outside the conditions, as forecast, had become treacherous. Staff were advised to avoid attempting to journey home if not absolutely necessary.

Nurse Miryam, for convenience, lived within walking distance, about twenty-five minutes from the hospital. She shared her modest two-roomed rental property with her aging mother. With home help and the cooperation of her two sisters, they ensured their mother had care twenty-four-seven.

A text message from the sister due to relieve their other sister, clutched Miryam by the throat. The first sister had left their mom's house early before the heaviest of the snowfall. But not until she was home did she get the news that the second sister had been caught in a snowdrift not far from the housing estate where she lived. She, in turn, had abandoned her car and returned home.

Miryam tried to call both sisters. She got through only to the first. She was preparing dinner for her family now. And besides, she was on the other side of the city. Had Miryam tried calling the care assistant?

"Right," Miryam said. "Thanks for your help. Not." She closed the call, her emotions conflicted.

Should she really have been so short with her sister? She wasn't sure. But, regardless, snapping at her the way she had injected into her system the fire she needed to make a decision. She went to her supervisor and told her she had to finish her shift a few hours early.

The supervisor tried to dissuade her. Especially in her condition. Wasn't there someone else, one of her mother's neighbours or someone, who could call in on her?

There wasn't. The truth was Miryam and her mother had been renting the two-bedroomed cottage for almost three years now, and they only knew one or two neighbours just to say 'hello' to.

"I'll be fine," she said. Hopefully her mom would be sleeping and wouldn't even realise she'd been on her own. She hated being alone.

Outside everything was coated in white. So thick did the snow lie on the ground, there were no cars on the roads. Had the circumstances been different, Miryam would have been filled with childish wonder. She had always loved the way snow covered everything up, made all the streets, the houses, the roads, every building and all the open spaces appear as though connected. No divisions were apparent. And the people too. Everyone saw the same images.

But now her focus was getting home to her mom. The freshly fallen snow was easy to walk on. There were places, however, like patches at bus stops and outside shops where footfall had been concentrated that were treacherous.

In what was considered a rough part of the city, a gang of teenage boys approached Miryam and asked her where she was going and what she was up to. She ignored them and tried to work her way around them. In vain. One of them, with a face too young for his tall and skinny frame, stepped in front of her, his arms held out cruciform. Between his lips a miserable looking cigarette. Unlit.

"Ah now, don't be like that," he said. "Be nice. All we want is a few cigarettes." He laughed a nasally laugh.

"I don't smoke," Miryam said.

"Not a bother," the pack leader said. "Give us your odds then." He extended his hand for the coins he expected. This time he didn't laugh. But the three or four others around him made sounds like a cackle of hyenas.

"Please," she said. "I'm expecting a baby." Inside her she felt contractions.

The skinny one looked about him and said something she couldn't understand.

Another explosion of laughter, full of threat and nastiness.

"Get her bag," the leader said to one of the others. He stood back, took out a box of matches, struck it and protected the flame in his cupped hands as he lit the stubby cigarette clamped between his teeth.

The jingle-jangle sound of bells tolling turned Miryam's tormentors' heads. Coming from a side road, the cushioned clip-clop of horses' hooves. Attached to the horse a carriage. In place of carriage wheels longitudinal runners. Up front was an old man holding the reins.

"Whoa there, Dasher. Whoa Prancer," the white-bearded figure said to his horses. Beneath the light thrown by a lamppost, he sat there looking at Miryam and the gang around her. On his face a wide smile. From the nostrils of one of his horses puffed plumes of steam. The other one hoofed the snowy ground.

The gang looked confused and waited a response from their leader.

"What do you want, old man?" he said.

The driver of the carriage laughed a three-syllabled laugh.

"Get lost and mind your own nose," the tall, skinny kid said. He jerked his thumb over his own shoulder.

"I'm here to give the lady a lift," the carriage driver said.

"Right, get him," the skinny leader said.

The teenage group rushed the carriage. A mistake. The driver used his whip to lash the air between them. This, and the sudden movement by the gang caused the pair of horses to rear up, lashing the air with their forelegs. One or two of the braver ones who tried to get around the side of the carriage were struck by the old man's whip.

"Come on. Scarper," the leader said to his gang as he held his arm where the whip had connected.

Off they went.

Next the old man was out of his carriage and helping Miryam off the snowy ground where she had sat down.

"My baby," she said. "I think he's coming." She pressed her hands to her front.

With the strength she'd never have expected in the old man, Miryam found herself being lifted off the ground and placed into a bed of straw in the carriage. Only when he asked her for her address did she realise that the gentleman could have been Mr Klaus, the elderly patient in the bed opposite the younger man. But probably it was her imagination and the weak state she was in.

Within seconds, it seemed like, she was outside her home. Quicker still, she was inside in the living room in front of the open hearth, where blazed a fire that filled the room with a heat that matched the way she felt. Kneeling beside her, Miryam's elderly mother held her hand and spoke to her in a lucid way she hadn't for so long. Her mom told her about the lovely man who had brought her home. But who had disappeared before she had time to thank him properly. Santos, her mom said he called himself.

Right now there were other things to attend to. Miryam's baby was on its way. She followed her mom's instructions to stop pushing once the baby's head was visible and to let nature do its work.

A relatively easy delivery, Miryam received the baby from her mom's arms and held it to her. Its sweet milky scent left her instantly intoxicated. Into its dark eyes she stared and felt that terrible and instant bond. Such was the ferocity of her love, she knew that she had loved this child forever. Long before its birth.

And then, while checking its tiny hands and feet, she saw curious markings. Birthmarks they looked like in the baby boy's palms and the bridges if his feet. Just like those of the bearded stranger in the hospital. And she knew now that young man's name. For it was her baby's name: Emmanuel.

About the author

Steve Wade's award winning short fiction has been widely published and anthologised. His stories have appeared in over fifty print publications, including Fjords, Boyne Berries, Crannog, Bridge House Publishing, New Fables, and Aesthetica Creative Works Annual. He has won First Prize in the Delvin Garradrimna Short Story Competition on four occasions. Winner of the Short Story category in the Write by the Sea writing competition 2019. He was a prize nominee for the PEN/O'Henry Award, and a prize nominee for the Pushcart Prize.

www.stephenwade.ie

Entranced

Margaret Bulleyment

30 Willow Rd
Lower Blackthorn
Oxon 25 4YR

20 October 2017

Dear Madame,
   I found the enclosed letter addressed to Marie, when I was sorting out the home of my late grandfather, Robert Miller. I do not know your relationship to him, although I do know he spent his childhood in France. I am sorry to tell you that he died in his sleep on 1st October at home in Oxfordshire, having celebrated his 100th birthday with his family – me and my son, Matty – just two weeks earlier. As you may know he was not religious, so we had him cremated in Oxford. I am so sorry that I did not find this letter earlier, so you could have known the arrangements. I can let you have more information when I know that this letter has reached you.
   My sincerest condolences,
   Emily Trafford

La Ferme Meunier
St. Paul des Roches
Avignon 35719
31 October 2017

Chère Emily,

Thank you for your letter informing me my brother, Robert Meunier is dead. Sadly, we lost touch many years ago, but I am very happy to know that I have more family members and that Robert ended his life peacefully with them.

I am ten years younger than Robert and not in good health (I am dictating this letter to my young farm manager and family friend, Jean-Luc) but I would like to invite you and your son to spend Christmas with me in Provence – before I join my late brother.

Our old family farm is now holiday cottages, so there is plenty of room for you to stay and explore where your grandfather was born and for us to get to know each other a little.

Jean-Luc is adding his details to this letter and will help you make the arrangements. You can email and message and all those things that young people do. Perhaps you have already made plans for Christmas but if not, an old lady would be very happy if you would accept this invitation.

Mes amitiés,

Marie (Meunier) leBrun

"There it is, there it is! Where's the other half… in the river? Can you run along it and jump in the water? Can I jump in the water? *Sur le pont d'Avignon…*"

"Not a good idea, Matty," said Jean-Luc slowing the car down, "anyway the bridge looks a lot better viewed from this side of the river, than if you're standing on it, or in the water."

"Put that seatbelt back on right now, Matty and sit still!" screamed Emily over the alarm buzzer.

"I'm sorry, Jean-Luc, Matty gets carried away sometimes. He loved the train, but the excitement of actually getting here is too much for him. He means well, but he has difficulties. To be honest, I wasn't going to accept Marie's invitation but Matty loved his great-grandfather, as I did and..."

"Don't apologise. I've told you not to worry. You'll be well away from the main house so Matty can make as much noise as he likes and no one will care. Now you're here, just relax. I'm impressed by Matty's French accent and the fact that he knows more than one verse of *Sur le pont.* He must have had a good teacher."

A good teacher who cannot control her own nine-year-old, thought Emily as the city disappeared behind them. Her headache was getting worse and the sky seemed impossibly blue and bright for December.

"We'll be at the farm in twenty minutes, Matty," Jean-Luc assured him.

Precisely twenty minutes later, Matty's watch bleeped. "Where's the farm? Where's the farm?"

"Just up the road and round the bend by those big rocks."

As the car slowed through the gates, Matty got more agitated. "That was twenty-one minutes and where's the big tree? Where's the big tree?"

"We had to have it felled. It got dangerously damaged in last month's storm."

Jean-Luc glanced at Emily. "How did...?"

"He saw the tree on the farm's website photo. He's been looking at it every day since he knew he we were coming here."

Matty was still chanting, "The tree's gone" as the car stopped in front of a large stone farmhouse with olive trees on sentry duty in battered pots outside the door. "That's where Marie lives," said Jean-Luc, "but for now I'll take you to your cottage and we'll get together later. You'll be eating with us of course at Marie's, not in the farm restaurant. I'll come and collect you at six. You'll probably want to catch up on your sleep before then."

Matty had not wanted to sleep but having explored every corner of the cottage, re-organising the kitchenette cupboards a spoon at a time had kept him amused until Jean-Luc returned.

"We're eating in the kitchen this evening," he said ushering Emily and Matty through the front door. "Marie will join us later."

Emily restrained herself from whipping out her phone and taking a photo of what any interior designer would kill for – a genuine Provencal kitchen complete with hanging strings of onions and herbs, giant pots and a battered wooden table large enough to feed a football team. There were three places laid and as they sat down an elderly lady lifted a huge tureen of soup brimming with vegetables, on to the table.

"Sylvie has looked after the Meuniers for years," said Jean-Luc, by way of introduction, handing round the bread basket, "but before we start, let's toast your arrival." He deftly uncorked the bottle on the table and poured Emily a glass. "It's local of course."

"Can I have some? It's as red as blood," said Matty bobbing up from his chair.

"I don't think that's…" Emily began.

"Of course, you can." Jean-Luc winked at Emily and poured a tiny measure into Matty's wineglass.

"Wait until we're all ready. Now together – Santé! Cheers!" He raised his glass to them.

"Ergh! That's horrible," said Matty, spitting it out. "It tastes like rusty old nails."

"That's how it should taste at your age, young man. Would you like some juice?"

Headache or not, Emily was more appreciative of the local produce than her son. This was the nearest she had got to relaxing all day.

"Everything's old inside, here," said Matty, rubbing his hand along the battered table top. "Our cottage is new inside."

"That's because our tourists love old Provence from the outside, but like their mod cons inside. But when of course we have more discerning visitors," Jean-Luc nodded towards Matty, "it's a different story. Tomorrow when it's light you can have a proper look around."

"I want to see the swimming pool and..." Matty stopped and looked towards the door. "Bonsoir, Madame," he called, jumping up and running to her. "Etes-vous m'arriere-grande-tante Marie? Bonsoir, bonsoir."

Emily turned to see an elegant old lady in blue, leaning on a walking stick. This was not the withered little old great-aunt she had imagined.

Matty was bouncing up and down in the front of the old lady, still bonsoiring her.

Marie took a step back and steadied herself against the door frame. "I am." She paused and stared at Matty. "This polite and handsome young man," she said quietly, "with those big brown eyes and shiny black hair, must be Matty. Your French accent is much better than my English one. Non? Do you have a kiss for your tante?"

Matty stepped back. "But you're not my aunt, you're..." he looked towards Emily in confusion.

"How about you just call me Marie?"

"Tante Marie will be fine," said Emily, coming forward.

Her great-aunt took a long look at her and kissed her on both cheeks. "Let's go through to my sitting room," she said taking Emily's arm.

Marie lead the way down a narrow corridor to a room, warm and bright from a glowing fire and a wall of ceiling to floor curtains in vibrant red and yellow patterns. Pointing Emily towards one of two huge sofas, Marie slowly lowered herself into a cushioned red chair beside a table covered with pills and bottles.

Matty ran straight in and hugged a curtain. "Sun colours."

"Careful, Matty," said Emily.

"Let's find something to play with," said Jean-Luc. "My laptop's in the other room."

"Thank you, but he has problems if he has too much screen time."

"Just a few minutes wouldn't…"

"What are these little people?" said Matty, running across the room to a huge wooden cabinet.

"Those are santons, Matty. Little saints," said Marie. "Terracotta painted figures from Christmas cribs. Years ago we had a complete family set, but that's all that's left now."

"Let's get them out of the cabinet and look at them, Matty, while your mum and Marie talk," said Jean-Luc. "Now this one's the miller – the family name Meunier, means Miller – did you know that?"

"He's got a donkey."

"He's got a donkey, he's covered in flour and he leads the dancing."

"There isn't a miller in the Christmas story," said Matty.

"A long time ago," said Jean-Luc, "churches in France were shut, so at Christmas when people couldn't see the church crib with Mary and Joseph, they made their own little figures. You can have anyone you want in your crib, but there are certain village people that are as important as the holy figures and the miller's one of them."

Matty sat down on the floor as Jean-Luc handed more figures down. "This is one of the kings, Matty – Balthazar – who's supposed to have stopped in Provence on his way from the Holy Land and stayed here forever."

"In France, not Jesus land?"

"It's a story, Matty, but the village he 'lived' in is near here and is very beautiful."

"Can we go there?"

"Yes, we could manage that."

Marie was watching Matty intently. "You have a lovely son, Emily."

"Yes. He can be difficult to deal with sometimes, he has…"

"Your grandfather was difficult. Not like Matty, but he was a very restless person and could be arrogant and angry when he wanted to be. At least that was how he seemed to me as a little girl."

"That doesn't sound like Grandpa."

"It was a long time ago and we were living in very difficult times."

"Grandpa never talked about France. Mum told me he was born here, but she knew nothing about his family and I was never taken to France as a child. My grandmother had died before I was born and Grandpa lived with us then, so we used to all go on holiday together – Scotland, Switzerland, Scandinavia. I grew up knowing a lot about northern fjells and fjords, but nothing about Grandpa's southern homeland."

"Jean-Luc said that you're a Spanish teacher."

"Yes and both my late parents were teachers too. I enjoyed languages at school and I thought that Grandpa would like me learning French, but he didn't. He just said there were more useful languages. When I had a choice between German or Spanish, as a second language, he told me German was for fools, but Spanish was the language of the sun – whatever that meant. Anyway Spanish became my first language and Grandpa was happy to encourage me speaking it."

"It was Spain that really changed Robert. I can remember him going – he would have been about nineteen, so I was Matty's age. He came back so angry – with himself – with us – with everyone. I don't know what he did out there – some kind of interpreter possibly – but what side he fought on, or what that involved, is a mystery even now."

"Fought? The Spanish Civil War?"

"Yes and later during the Occupation here, he took what he had learned in Spain, to the maquis."

"The Resistance?"

"Yes, but remember, here we were also occupied by our own – the Vichy government. Your neighbour could be a more likely enemy, than someone in a uniform speaking a foreign language. You never knew where peoples' sympathies lay and most of the time you didn't want to know. I was old enough by then to understand what was happening. Robert would just disappear for days on end. My dad was an olive farmer and needed all the help he could get, not someone who disappeared for guns and explosives."

"Grandpa was a history lecturer. I can't imagine him doing any of those things."

"Doing what?" called Matty. "Jean-Luc is going to take us to see where one of the three kings lived."

"That's very kind of him, but we mustn't get in the way of his proper work."

"It's fine," said Marie. "Jean-Luc's job is to look after you while you're here. We've plenty of staff over Christmas."

"We could go to Les Baux, tomorrow," said Jean-Luc. "It gets crowded this near Christmas, but we could have lunch there and then you can come back and explore the farm. Anyway, let me escort you back to your cottage now, you must be tired."

Jean-Luc and Emily trailed Matty as he danced along the illuminated path singing *We Three Kings*.

"Don't get me wrong," said Emily, "you've been very helpful organising this visit for us and I'm very grateful and pleased that you get on well with Matty – lots of people can't cope – but don't assume he's like any nine-year-old – he isn't – and there are certain things that he can't do, so please don't undermine me in dealing with him."

"Relax, Emily. Let Matty be himself, not someone with difficulties and problems and all the other things you expect him to have. He'll surprise you yet."

"And I suppose your one day knowledge of him, is superior to my years of parenthood?"

"You're tired. I'll be back at eight tomorrow morning. Goodnight, Matty."

"Are we going all the way up there? It's fortress in the sky!" Matty squirmed in his car seat.

"If you take that seat belt off, Matty, we go straight back," shouted Emily.

"It's a village perche. The citadel and the village are built on a 'bau' a high rocky... I don't know the English word," said Jean-Luc.

"Ridge? Escarpment? It's very impressive, whatever it's called," Emily admitted.

The moment the car was parked, Matty was out of it, dancing on the spot. "We're going up, we're going up."

"Only a little way up to the village," Jean-Luc whispered to Emily, as they began the steep ascent through the narrow stone streets.

"What's that lovely smell?" Matty shouted, darting ahead of them in spite of the crowds.

"The Christmas market," bellowed Jean-Luc. "Would you like some pain d'espice – gingerbread? If you want some you'd better wait for us up there."

Later perched on a rocky seat, Matty waved his half-eaten gingerbread over the ramparts, "From here you can see people coming from miles away."

"That's exactly what the mediaeval warriors, who lived up here like eagles, thought too," said Jean-Luc. He turned to Emily. "Can you believe they were the same people who founded the troubadour Court of Love? How's that for war and peace," he laughed. "Santon Museum, Matty?"

The tiny building built into the rock was crammed with people, but the moment Matty had squeezed through the door, he stood entranced in front of the very first tableau. "It's not a stable, it's a cave with rocks and bushes and these kings have got camels and the shepherds, sheep and it's beautiful. Can we make a cave for our santons? There's plenty of rocks at the farm."

"Come and look at these figures, Matty," Emily called. "They're very old and it looks like they're made of glass."

"I like these ones the best. Their clothes are all different. The kings have robes, the shepherds have patches and the little man holding his arms up and staring at the baby Jesus, has trousers and braces. Isn't that funny? Let's stay here and look at them."

"But someone is waiting to meet you up near the church, Matty," said Jean-Luc. "I've told my sister how interested you are in santons and she just happens to make them. She wants to meet you and show you her workshop. Shall we go?"

"Up we go, up we go," Matty danced off behind Jean-Luc.

"Welcome Matty and Emily to *Santons Forel*. I'm Françoise. Please follow me."

She smiles like her brother, thought Emily as they squeezed through the busy shop, past shelves of painted santons and piles of boxes to the workshop, where rows of tiny figures were lined up waiting to be fired. "These are the last of this year's figures, Matty – washerwomen; chestnut sellers, fishermen and drummers."

"They're all blue and white."

"All my santons are blue and white this year."

"Like the sky and the clouds?"

"Exactly, Matty. Jean-Luc, perhaps you and Emily would like a drink while I show Matty how I make a figure?"

"We would. See you later."

"I'm glad Matty's enjoying his Provencal Christmas," said Jean-Luc, stirring his coffee vigorously.

"Forgive me asking Emily, but you don't celebrate with Matty's dad?"

"No. He's had nothing to do with us since Matty was little. He's Spanish. I think Marie realised that. I met Paolo teaching in Cordoba. We were never married but – call me old-fashioned – I'd hoped that would happen after Matty was born. But when Paolo realised Matty was, in his word 'handicapped', he left."

"And you think if Matty had not been born 'Matty', he would have stayed?"

"Maybe, but I can't blame Matty for him leaving, can I? Do you have children?"

"No. Sadly, my marriage failed. I wanted to stay here, have children and help Marie develop the farm, but Yvette thought we should move on and take our talents to the States, or Australia, or anywhere that wasn't here. She thought that wanting to stay where you grew up, was some kind of weakness."

"I'm sorry – who wouldn't want to stay in such a lovely place, especially when it's your home. That's why I find

75

Grandpa's life so difficult to understand. I also need to apologise for what I said to you last night, but now that Grandpa's no longer my support with Matty, I feel people are judging me all the time."

"Well they're not, so just relax and…"

"I love it here." Matty emerged from the workshop, clutching a plastic bag. "Francoise has shown me how she makes and paints the little people," he enthused. "I've started making my own santon."

"Wonderful, Matty," said Emily. "Thank you so much, Francoise. I hope we haven't taken up too much of your time."

"No, I've enjoyed it. He shows promise as a model maker. Goodbye Matty and give my love to Marie."

"I'm looking for rocks as soon as we get back," Matty decided on the return journey. "Where's the best place to look?"

"Right outside our cottage, said Emily, "where I can see you."

"I'll look for a little table and some wood we can put the figures on," said Jean-Luc, "then we can get started this evening."

After dinner, Emily left Jean-Luc and Matty spreading a plastic sheet over the kitchen floor, while she went to find Marie in her sitting room.

"I hear Matty is very interested in reviving the family's santon tradition," said Marie.

"He's had a wonderful day – and so have I. What a beautiful part of the world this is. I can't believe Grandpa never talked about it."

"He never saw the beauty of it, only the brutality of the times and that stayed with him. The last time we sat down to what we thought was our usual Provencal family Christmas, was 1943. Food was not plentiful even here, but we had our santons and we hoped the family – me and my parents, your grandfather and your great-uncle, Louis – was going to be together."

"Louis?"

"Louis was two years younger than me and he was… like Matty. When I saw Matty, I couldn't believe it."

"You mean…?"

"In those days, no one talked of social difficulties, or spectrums, you were what you were and everyone took that for granted – perhaps that was better. Robert was especially protective of Louis and if some of the village lads were a bit cruel to him they had Robert to answer to, but most people accepted him for what he was. He'd plenty of friends and he was always safe with them.

"Like Matty, he was very bright, but very innocent. He was also an incredible athlete who could run, throw and jump like no one else. The maquis often used younger lads to help them – they were quicker, agile and more dextrous than older ones – and the lads wanted to impress their heroes.

"One local group realised how useful Louis could be and started to secretly train him up. Robert was away in Marseilles at the time, my parents were busy struggling with the farm and I had no idea what was happening.

"On Christmas Eve, we were preparing our traditional meal waiting for Louis to appear. Robert we never wondered about – he came and he went – but we hoped he would respect the family tradition. He did. He appeared out of nowhere – but Louis did not. Robert said he would go and look for him, but before he'd stepped out of the door, there was an explosion from somewhere down towards Avignon.

"Robert rushed out and returned after midnight in a dreadful state, crying and covered in mud and blood.

"I'd never seen Robert cry. He told us Louis was dead, but justice had been done. That's all he said.

"Then he started gathering clothes, food and whatever he'd hidden in the barns and he left again. That was the last time we ever saw him."

"But... that's more than seventy years go. How could he...?"

"We thought Robert was dead too. Later we heard all sorts of rumours – the group's leader Michel Forel, had trained Louis to throw a grenade at some important convoy disguised as an ambulance and it all went wrong. Much later we found that Louis having thrown the grenade, ran towards the convoy, not away from it. Was he confused that it was an ambulance? We'll never know. Michel also died that evening. My family mourned the loss of Robert and the Forels mourned their son too.

"Forel? But that's..."

"Michel was Jean-Luc's great-uncle. My parents and I couldn't get out of our heads what Robert had said before he left. Had Michel just died in the confusion, like Louis, or had Robert killed him?"

"So you're telling me that Grandpa might have killed Jean-Luc's great-uncle? This is..."

"There's more. Dad had employed a young man called Nicholas LeBrun to help run the farm – to do what Robert had never done. Nicholas was a lovely man and we married after the war. My parents died – they never recovered from losing Louis and Robert – and Nicholas and I took over the farm. We sadly never had children of our own and we realised in the sixties that the farm was struggling and we'd be better off making a living through tourism. We tried to keep it looking like a farm and it's been successful – especially since Jean-Luc joined us – although I wonder what my parents would make of it now.

One summer twenty years after I had last seen Robert, a postcard arrived from Granada – no message, just a letter

'R' on it. After that a postcard arrived every summer – from Switzerland, Norway, Scotland – but never – and I didn't think about it at the time – England. They all had the same 'R' on them, Robert had to be alive. When they stopped arriving, I assumed he was dead."

"But how could he not visit his own flesh and blood so long after the war was over?"

"In his letter, Robert told me all about your grandmother, your mother, you and Matty. He said how like Louis Matty was. He also told me that he didn't mean to kill Michel, but he wanted to punish him for using Louis in the way he did. His anger got violently out of control and Michel died. Robert felt that his life had ended too and he did some very reckless things afterwards, just wanting to be killed – but it never happened.

Then he realised he had the opportunity to redeem himself, by beginning all over again. His rebirth was so much happier than he could have imagined, but he could never return here. He was sorry for the pain he'd caused the family, but it was best for everyone."

"It's nearly all set up, Mum," said Matty bursting into the room. "Jean-Luc has shown me where the figures go. The wise man has to be further away because he doesn't get there until later. Why are you crying?"

"That's wonderful, Matty," interrupted Marie, "because tomorrow night we have our Christmas Eve dinner – Le Gros Souper – our first proper family one for years and you can add the final touches to the crib." She looked at Emily. "Would you like to go to the village church? We don't go but…"

"No, Marie. A family Christmas dinner is all we need and thank you so very much for what you've shared with me. It must be very painful for you."

"Marie's told you everything, hasn't she?" said Jean-Luc, as they followed Matty back to the cottage.

"Yes, but it hasn't sunk in yet. The strange thing is that Matty who was so close to his GG, has not mentioned him once since we arrived and coming to see where Grandpa was born was the reason we came."

"Perhaps he can't imagine his great-grandfather being a child like him."

"Any more than I can imagine him killing your relative?"

"I don't think we bear any grudges. That sounds like a bad joke. Goodnight, Emily. I'll see you both tomorrow evening. Don't expect turkey and Christmas pudding, Matty."

On his return the following evening, Jean-Luc found Matty outside the cottage door, scrubbing a huge rock. "Look what I've found, Jean-Luc. The best rock ever for our crib. It's got a hole in it big enough for the stable cave. We haven't got a baby Jesus, but I…"

"Matty put that down and get in the shower now," said Emily appearing at the door. "I'm so sorry J… No, I'm not. Forget the apology – you know what Matty's like. I'm going to relax." She laughed.

"Laughing and relaxing suit you better than apologising, especially in the lamplight," joked Jean-Luc.

A well-scrubbed Matty finally arrived at the farmhouse door. "We were going to eat in the dining room," said Marie, but Jean-Luc persuaded me that you'd rather be in the kitchen with your crib. Whatever's that?"

"Half an escarpment by the weight of it," said Jean-Luc, lifting Matty's rock on to the corner table, "but that's the cave for our crib. We'll deal with it later."

"What are all these things on the table and why are there three cloths?" said Matty. "I'm not going to be that messy."

"This is our version of Le Gros Souper, Matty," said Marie. "These are all traditional things connected with the

Christmas story. It's a simple meal followed by thirteen desserts. So let's have our soup and fish and then we'll explain them."

"Can I just have the desserts?"

"No, Matty," said Emily, "you need…"

"Let him have what he wants," said Marie firmly. "He's the one who has brought Christmas back to life for us."

"I'll get my crib ready," said Matty.

After several reprises of *We Three Kings*, from the santon corner, Marie finally announced, "It's time for the desserts. Now, Matty, there's fruit bread; almonds; raisins; figs; walnuts; white nougat; black nougat; almond candies; dates and three kinds of fresh fruit."

"That's twelve," said Matty.

"Well, we've cheated a bit," said Jean-Luc, as Sylvie slid bowls of glistening cake on to the table.

"This is a 'gateau des rois' – the candied fruits are the jewels of the three kings – and it's eaten after Christmas," said Marie, "but especially for you, we're eating it on Christmas Eve."

"Careful, Matty, because you never know what's hidden in it," added Jean-Luc. "The good news is that if you find something, you're King for a Day."

Matty prodded his cake gingerly. "There's something hard in it." He put his fingers into the bowl. "It's a… baby Jesus… and it's blue and white."

"It's the last figure you add to your crib on Christmas Eve," said Jean-Luc.

"If it's the last, I have two more to put in first," said Matty reaching into his pocket. "I tried to make my santon with his arms in the air like the one in the museum, but he came out lop-sided. Then I found that rock and look what was inside it." He held up a painted wooden santon clad in a long nightshirt, with its arms uplifted.

"Le ravi," whispered Marie. "It's the most important figure. 'The one who is entranced' – an innocent person who has woken up and is overwhelmed by the cave scene in front of him. Your great-grandfather carved that figure for his younger brother."

"GG made this?"

Matty placed the figure in front of the cave. "That's for GG. I miss him."

Marie took Emily's hand. "I want you to know that I'm leaving the farm to you. You're my only family and I know that you and Matty will take care of it and will love it like I do."

"That's unbelievably generous, Marie but I don't know anything…"

"But Jean-Luc does and it's yours – provided he remains the manager. All three of you will bring new life to this place."

"If you can stand it, Emily, so can I," laughed Jean-Luc, raising his glass. "Santé!"

"Santé!" echoed Emily. "Put the baby in the crib, King Matty."

"Can I lick the cake off him first?"

About the author

Margaret Bulleyment began writing fiction and plays, after a long career in comparative education. She has had short stories published in anthologies, including Bridge House's *Café Lit*, *Snowflakes*, *Baubles*, *Glit-er-ary* and *Crackers,* and on story websites.

As a finalist in the Ovation Theatre Awards, she has twice had short plays performed professionally. Her children's play *Caribbean Calypso* was runner-up in Trinity College of Music and Drama's 2011 International Playwriting Competition and is available on TreePress. In December 2017 the play was performed three times in Bangalore, India by Jagriti Kids – a charity promoting literacy and school attendance.

Fathering

L F Roth

"Life's so predictable," she said, across the kitchen table.

Although she didn't quite face me, her tone warned me not to challenge her. I was still tempted. There was nothing predictable about my being there. Her dog was the cause. A St. Bernard.

"People die."

True enough.

She'd had problems holding him. "Dogs on heat," she had disclosed. "He goes wild." She'd given him Monk's pepper. "An anti-aphro…" The word tripped her up; not unduly concerned, she left it hanging.

Before me arose an ancient monastery, stone upon stone, the monks in their cells, their eyes dead. I'd grabbed his lead and yanked him back. It was not without an effort that I walked the two of them home, guided by her instructions.

"People die," she repeated.

I nodded. I'd turned down a drink, but she'd had me join her anyway. While she poured hers, I cleared the table, letting the dishes that had accumulated join those in the sink. Everywhere were plants folding up on themselves.

"Anyone close?" I asked.

"My mother. Seventy-two this year."

I offered my condolences.

Her lips trembled. "Why?" she moaned. "Why? Why?"

The dog howled.

She lifted her glass and put it down half empty. The dog tilted its head.

"Three years after Jerry," she remarked. "It feels like yesterday. When he died she saved everything, as if that would bring him back. Everything. She even kept his clothes, hoping against hope that Jacqui would have a son. She knew I wouldn't."

I thought it best not to comment.

"What good are they now?"

"Your father," I queried.

"Jacqui's."

I waited. Not that it was any of my business.

She disappeared into her glass, mumbling to herself.

"The place is a mess," she added. "There are my mother's things, too. Clothes. Books. Records. Cassettes. Video tapes. Bet you can't guess what she bought last year."

I didn't try.

"A second-hand loom. At seventy! She, who'd never knitted so much as a scarf. She had an idea she could make a runner out of what Liston shed."

"Liston?"

"The dog. Jerry got it for her. He named it Sonny, but she favoured Liston. Like the boxer. They had the same jawline."

I studied the dog. Poor boxer.

"Of course, Jacqui wants to get rid of it all."

"But you don't?"

"I'd like to go through it first."

"Jerry. Jacqui. Liston. And you?"

It took a moment before she caught on. "Oh. Mel."

"Melinda? Melanie? Melissa?"

"Mel."

I smiled. "Frank." And having introduced myself, I left.

But only to return. I gave Mel a past, adding to what her appearance and the state of her flat suggested. In the mid-nineties, I'd seen her in a local pub, though not to talk to. She'd been with an older crowd, a rough one, and I with mine – she had a few years on me. While I had drifted on, for her, life must have remained much the same. Now I was settled in the old neighbourhood again and calling by on my way home from work became something of a habit.

On each occasion, her flat had grown more cluttered. Books and cassette tapes kept piling up; clothes that had belonged to her mother hung from door knobs and chairs; a scuffed chest of drawers blocked much of the entrance to the kitchen until she found room for it by shuffling things around, placing on its top a standard lamp and a stool – the lamp horizontal, the stool upside down. Bending over to wipe Sonny's feet after a walk – I preferred Sonny to Liston – I glimpsed boxes of kitchenware under her bed.

"So where's the loom?" I ventured.

She laughed. Sonny smiled.

"Jacqui will be happy to dispose of it. In most ways she's as careless as a teenager, but not if there is money involved. A good thing, you might say; she's thirty-three. Mum had some Wedgwood pottery and it was gone in the blink of an eye." A grimace dismissed the whole business. "Well, she was her mother too. At any rate, it's not worth squabbling over."

"She'll sell it?"

A nod.

"And you?"

"Me?"

Would she try and sell what she had brought was what I meant. But that was not her intention.

"I'll keep some. The rest I just want to go over."

Her mother's old dresses? Books and tapes? Why?

But that was what she did.

It seemed so casual at first that I hardly noticed. She would put on a tape and play both sides from start to finish, barely listening to what was there – recordings from the radio, mostly. The same with videos. With books she would afford each page no more than a glance, as if to merely check that none had been torn out or scribbled on. It was only when she turned a coat inside out to trace the lining with her thumb and fingers that I saw that there was method in what appeared madness.

"You after anything special?" I asked.

Now, had she been a child, the likely answer would have been: "Oh, no." And she would have tossed the coat aside as of no interest.

But though she struck me as childlike at times, she wasn't evasive.

"My father," she announced.

I could have made a joke of it but didn't.

"Your father?" I echoed.

And she explained.

I put my arm around her the moment she fell silent – she was clutching her mother's coat. There was a faraway look in her eyes.

I probed her. "Not even a first name?"

But she had been told nothing. "He was a mistake," was all her mother had revealed. Not whether they had seen each other only once or spent weeks or even months together. Not how they had met. Nor what he did. Nothing. Not a word. Not even what had made him a mistake. This must have been in 1969.

Flower power. Drugs. Rock 'n' roll.

A world that ended before either of us had reached school age.

"Forget it," her mother had instructed her.

But how do you go about forgetting something you never knew?

"I used to daydream," she revealed later, in bed – for that was where my hug took us.

For my part, I'd been so conscious of the implements that stuck up from the boxes beneath us that I'd found it hard to perform. Was there a set of sharpened carving knives aimed at me? A meat axe that had landed on top of pots and pans, its edge pointing upwards? No doubt her past got in the way, too, not in the form of knives, perhaps, but through thoughts brought to the surface by her search. We used the right phrases; we made the right sounds, yet the bed felt like a stage.

"I fantasized. One of my teachers was my father. He had come back for me. Any day now he'd whisk me off and take me... somewhere. I must have been eight or nine. I made up to him – there is no other word for it – until I learned he had a daughter, one my age. Oh, how I hated her! Then, at the end of the year, he resigned. That left a gap but made my life easier."

She broke off.

"There were others," she added. "A neighbour, for a spell; the postman. But there's no need to go into that. Later, my fantasies became more abstract. My father was a film star; a famous guitarist; a scientist. Each had a career to pursue, which accounted for his absence. The mistake was my mother's, not seeing where his true passion lay. She was at fault, not whoever she'd let father her child."

She turned to face me.

"Of course, as often as not I blamed myself."

My fingers had been wandering. They stopped.

"For what?"

"For scaring him off."

"The idea of you?"

"No. But he may have been there to welcome me into the world – a child given life by accident. And had to face what? A baby bawling day and night. The smell of dirty nappies everywhere. Who would put up with that?"

"In that case you should follow your mother's advice. If he abandoned you, he's not worth bothering about. Stick to your fantasies. There you can make him anything you want." I swung my legs over the side of the bed. "Sonny needs to go out. I'll take him and then I must be off."

"For your next world tour."

"That's it. The life of a roadie. The band needs me." I gathered my clothes from the floor. "Here, Sonny," I called. "Let's get dressed."

And Sonny got up, stretched and shook his head, the slime flying everywhere. What newborn baby could top that?

In spite of all, Mel persevered.

I tried logic, but to no avail. If her mother had refused to tell her anything, why would she leave a hidden message? And why on tape? Besides, cassettes were only just coming into use in the seventies.

Her face expressed contempt for my naivety. "People say one thing and do another," she informed me. "That's something you can almost count on." She pressed the release button to turn the tape over. Some classic piece I vaguely recognized. Beethoven? An unintended link to Sonny? "And as for when, she could have made a recording later. Once I'd moved out. Or after Jerry died. Any time, in fact."

I hadn't thought of that. But why complicate matters, using a tape?

"She didn't keep a diary?"

A headshake.

"Did she have a PC? A pad? A mobile phone?"

More headshakes.

"She must have had a photo album, though?"

"No. She stored some folders in one of the top drawers. Her parents' wedding. That sort of thing."

I gestured towards the chest, to direct her there. "So?"

"Uh-uh." She made a face. "Mum taught me to always save the best for last. The mushrooms on a pizza. The pineapple in a fruit salad. I'll get there by and by."

How could I not love her?

There followed more days of Mel's flipping through the pages of books for notes or letters that might have been tucked away. This was fairly rapid work. Meanwhile, I rearranged what was in the boxes under the bed, just in case. Meat cleavers there were none. The clothes she also disposed of quickly, handing them in to a local charity I'd found for the books. The tapes took longer. She had to let them run from beginning to end, since a message could have been inserted anywhere. Being of no interest in themselves, they filled the function basically of background music. Not surprisingly, these searches led nowhere.

Mel eyed the chest of drawers, visibly tense. All paraphernalia was gone. The stool and the standard lamp had been returned to their places.

"It's quite impressive." I counted the drawers: three the whole width; four half-sized; eight quarter-sized. A total of fifteen. "At what end are you going to start?"

"Down the bottom. That's where she used to store bed linen. Above were the towels, tablecloths and napkins. None of them will hold any surprises."

"Hoping to find what?"

She gave me a tired look. "You know what."

"But more specifically?"

The silence built.

"A letter," she said finally. "From my mother. Marked 'Not to be opened until after my death'. Explaining everything. Who he was. What happened. What the mistake was. And whose."

"And failing that?"

"Can't you just let me get on with it?"

"One from your father?" I suggested. "'To my son or daughter if I had one'?"

"No. What would I learn from that?"

I gave her a hug. "Sorry. I didn't mean to pester you. But…" I broke off. Why lecture her? "I'll leave you to it. I'll take Sonny for a walk."

Which was what I had planned to do.

Sonny is a slow walker. Had he been stationed in the Alps, in no way would he have been assigned rescue work, intent, as he is, on following in the footsteps of other dogs, specifically those on heat. We were gone for over two hours. I'd left his towel hanging over the banister and wiped his feet and undercarriage before I pushed the door open.

Mel was sitting by the table. Behind her a drawer was open – the second from the left in the top row she had indicated as the place of a few folders. She had been crying.

"Any luck?" I asked.

She handed me a picture that lay in front of her, a somewhat faded colour print.

The man smiled at me. Around twenty-five, with his long hair, he could have been taken for a hippie, but the Ben Sherman shirt he wore spoke against this. Maybe his orange flared cords did, too – a bright note, if a little less intense with the passage of time.

I passed it back without turning it over. I didn't have to.

"You've got his eyes," I pointed out. "Was there a note with it?"

She frowned. "He's so young," she commented.

"Was. By now he will be in his seventies. If he is alive today. There was nothing else?"

"Nothing." She sighed. "I wish there had been a name.

90

It would have made him less anonymous. Andrew. Brian. Joe. Anything would do."

"Then pick one of them. Joe might not be far off."

"Joe," she repeated. "Yes. Why not. Joe. I'll get a frame tomorrow. There'll be no hiding him any more. He's to go on the wall. I wonder where, though. What do you think, Sonny?"

Sonny raised his ears briefly.

I congratulated myself. I had made a wise choice. My uncle had been a good man and it showed, I thought, in the photograph.

"A drink?" I proposed. "To celebrate?"

She pushed the drawer to and went to get two glasses. And ceremoniously, the photo still between us, we drank to Joe, in silence on my part.

Joseph, if one was to be quite correct.

About the author

L. F. Roth has had stories published in competition anthologies brought out by Biscuit Publishing, Earlyworks Press, Bridge House Publishing, Cinnamon Press, AudioArcadia.com, Momaya Press, University of Huddersfield Press, The Plymouth Writers Group, Black Pear Press and Hammond House. They generally focus on relationships, gender issues and trauma – at times all three. For details and a few excerpts, see https://sites.google.com/site/lfroth1.

Following the Star

Dawn Knox

How they had the nerve to call themselves *Three Wise Men*, Wing Lee had no idea.

Yes, there were three of them – and true, they were men... but not one of them could be described as *wise*...

According to Wing Lee, the sum total of their intelligence would not have produced sufficient energy to ignite a firecracker.

And yet, they were the masters and he was the servant.

Life was not fair.

The Three Wise Men had set off on an epic expedition to an undisclosed destination in the far west and they had engaged Wing Lee to manage a group of slaves during the journey. However, not long after they started out, one by one, every man, woman and child had been sold, and only Wing Lee remained. Since the finances were in such a mess, he wasn't receiving wages, which meant he was now as good as a slave.

Had Wing Lee been in charge of the funds on the expedition, he knew there would still be money in the coffer.

In fact, there would still *be* a coffer.

But it had been sold to replace the money which had been squandered by Wing Lee's masters during the early part of the trip. Indeed, by the time they left Samarkand, the reserves had started to run low which wasn't surprising since his masters had taken advantage of all the delights of the city and no expense had been spared. Well, no expense had been spared on the masters. Wing Lee and the slaves had not stayed in the finest hostelries – they had to make do with whatever they could find which usually meant the stables.

And as for the money spent on the gifts... Wing Lee would have had much more idea than his master, Caspar, who'd been sent out to purchase the items they would need. 'Canny Caspar', as he was known because of his alleged entrepreneurial skills, turned out to be good at striking a bargain but not so good at choosing gifts appropriate to the birth of a child. He'd returned to the Samarkand Palace Hotel with bolts of silk, precious gems, gold ingots, a jewel-encrusted sword, chests of costly spices, mysterious contraptions and two lions.

Caspar had, indeed, driven a hard bargain and his fellow wise men, Balthazar and Melchior had been impressed with the amount of money he'd saved, although that night, they'd lost it all at the gaming table.

They'd left Samarkand soon after.

Wing Lee hadn't known whether it was because of the immense bill his masters had run up in the hotel, or because the lions, which had escaped during the night, had mauled the hotel proprietor.

Anyway, it was just as well they'd left because they'd seriously misjudged the length of time it would take to get to their destination. They'd also seriously misjudged the location of their destination. And that was Melchior's fault.

He was the dreamer of the three, and the expedition had been his idea. He'd invited Caspar to accompany him because of his legendary financial shrewdness and also Balthazar because he was a formidable warrior which is how he'd earned his epithet – Balthazar the Bold. He was tall, broad and fearless although his one weakness was travel sickness when riding a camel, which currently rendered him useless as a guard. The route Melchior had chosen took them through vast stretches of desert and Wing Lee was beginning to doubt his master was as certain of their position as he led them to believe. It meant they travelled on their camels for

93

hours at a time and Balthazar showed very little evidence of getting used to the lurching motion.

And he wasn't the only one who was irritated by the endless sand dunes. Having had the wisdom to foresee that hours riding a camel might cause unpleasant chafing, Caspar had designed a device he'd called the Comfo-Saddle and he was testing it out. It was a veritable feat of engineering – being stable, durable and adjustable. It might even have been comfortable if he'd remembered the tools he would need to adjust it. It turned out that a badly-fitting Comfo-Saddle causes more rubbing and abrasion than an ordinary saddle.

Several months after they'd set out, Melchior, who was in the lead, held up a hand for the caravan to stop. On their right, in the distance, a range of mountains rose up like jagged teeth but other than that, sand stretched in all directions as far as the eye could see.

Despite the early hour, heat waves had begun to make the sand shimmer and dance, promising another scorching day. Each morning, they rose before dawn and travelled while the sun was still low. At Melchior's signal, they stopped, and Wing Lee erected the tents and prepared food while his masters rested, then later, when the sun began to dip towards the western horizon, Wing Lee would dismantle the tents and repack the camels, ready for them to set off again.

"I beg your pardon, sir," Wing Lee said to Melchior as he helped him off his camel, "but do you anticipate reaching civilisation or at least an oasis within the next few days? We're running short of water."

"Short of water?" Melchior was appalled. "D'you mean to tell me there'll be less water in my bath than there was yesterday?"

"I'm afraid there will be no bath today, sir. Nor tomorrow. Not until we find a source of water."

"That's preposterous, Wing Lee!"

"Indeed, it is, sir."

"How's a man to wash?"

"I'm afraid it's a stark choice, sir, you either smell… or you die. Oh, and we will also need to replenish our food stocks as soon as possible."

The two other wise men had not been happy when they discovered that food and water was being rationed.

"How much further until we reach civilisation?" Caspar asked. "I only joined the expedition to find new clients. Since we left Samarkand, we've hardly seen anyone. It's not good enough, Melchior! This isn't what you promised!"

"And I need time with my feet on the ground. When we've finished this trip, I don't ever want to see another camel," said Balthazar.

"Oh, stop complaining! I expect we'll find a town or village soon," said Melchior.

"What d'you mean *you expect*? Don't you know for certain?" asked Balthazar.

"Well, not exactly. But we're in the general vicinity…"

"*General vicinity?* There's nothing as far as the eye can see! And," said Balthazar. "I seem to remember that chain of mountains was on our left yesterday."

"So, what? There are mountains all over the place," said Melchior.

"Yes, but when they're on our left on one day and then on our right the next, it means that either the mountains have moved or we're zigzagging across the desert."

"Nonsense!" said Melchior, his eyes wide in alarm.

"Wing Lee! Bring the maps," shouted Balthazar.

The servant appeared with a rolled-up papyrus which he opened out on the table.

"I said *maps*," said Balthazar. "Where are the others?"

"We sold them just outside Samarkand, sir," said Wing Lee, "to buy supplies."

"You dimwit, Wing Lee!" said Balthazar. "Didn't it occur to you we'd need the maps to reach our destination?"

"Indeed, it did, sir, that's exactly what I told Mr Melchior, when he ordered me to sell them."

"Ah!" said Melchior. "Yes, well, I'm sure we'll manage admirably with this map."

Caspar, turned the map one way and then the other, "So, where are we? There are very few details marked. In fact, if I didn't know better, I'd assume this was a blank piece of papyrus with a few doodles on it."

Melchior peered at the map and nibbled his bottom lip.

"If I may be so bold, sir," said Wing Lee, "considering the direction of the sun, and the position of that mountain range, I believe we may be about here..." He indicated a large area in the middle of the map.

"That seems to make sense," said Balthazar. "Now, where are we making for?"

"Well, *obviously*, I won't know until tonight," said Melchior as if talking to a child.

"Because?" asked Balthazar.

"Because I can't see the star until night time."

"Star?"

"Yes, the star we're following."

"I thought you were navigating with that small, shiny thing you keep in your pocket. You're always getting it out and looking through it," said Caspar.

"Small, shiny thing?" asked Melchior, a puzzled frown on his face. "Oh! You mean this!" he said, taking a round piece of polished metal from his pocket and holding it up. "I don't look through it. I look into it. It's a mirror."

Neither Caspar nor Balthazar could speak.

"Trust me," said Melchior, "I'm as keen as you chaps to find civilisation. Not having enough water for a bath is intolerable."

Balthazar finally found his voice, "So, all this time, you've been checking your appearance and we've been following a *star?*"

"Oh yes."

"Which star?"

"Well, I don't know its name!" Melchior said crossly. "It comes up over in that direction." He waved his finger at the mountains.

"But, yesterday, the mountains were on our left," said Balthazar.

"I can't help that," said Melchior.

"How will we know when we've arrived?" asked Caspar.

"Because the star will stop," said Melchior.

"Stop what?" asked Balthazar, his hands palm up in a gesture of exasperation. "Stars don't do a great deal except twinkle. And if it stops twinkling, how will you know where it is?"

"You're being very childish," said Melchior. "The star's led us safely this far, hasn't it?"

Melchior was the first to wake up after his nap.

"I was wondering, sir, if we are going to head in *that* direction?" Wing Lee asked, his finger indicating the horizon near the last mountain in the range.

"Umm…"

"Only I've noticed the camels are all pointing in that direction and I know they can smell water over very long distances, so I thought perhaps…" said Wing Lee.

"Over in that direction, did you say?" asked Melchior.

"Yes, sir,"

"Well, that is indeed, where I was planning to take us."

They'd reached the village the following day and Wing Lee had queued with the women at the well, to replenish their water supply, listening to their chatter. He found out that Jerusalem wasn't many days' ride away and although none of the women had heard of the birth of a new prince, it was quite likely that one had been born and news hadn't yet reached their village.

"That's more like it!" said Caspar when Wing Lee conveyed the news about Jerusalem. "There'll be lots of networking to be done there."

"A city! At last!" said Balthazar. "With paved streets and proper buildings... We can find a luxury hotel..."

"And there'll be public baths!" said Melchior. "And I simply must get my hair trimmed."

Wing Lee cleared his throat, "If I may make so bold, kind sirs... we may need to make a few adjustments to expectations, if we are ever to get home again."

"What d'you mean?" asked Melchior.

"Well, sir, it has cost quite a lot to get this far, so it's only fair to assume we're going to require a similar amount to get home. And since we've sold most of our assets..."

"He has a point," said Caspar, "so, how shall we economise?"

Wing Lee crept out of the tent. He'd warned them about their extravagance. How they arranged to cut back on the spending, was up to them. There would undoubtedly be a heated discussion and Wing Lee feared it might get physical.

The brawl had finally ended when the tent collapsed on top of the three men who had to be disentangled by Wing Lee. It was decided that by the time the tent had been re-erected, it would be time to take it down. So, Wing Lee was told to pack up and they would set off earlier than usual for Jerusalem.

The journey passed in silence. Melchior had a black eye which he inspected periodically in his pocket mirror, Caspar had a split lip and Balthazar nursed his cut and bruised fist between intermittent bouts of vomiting.

King Herod, hearing that the three men had travelled from the East, granted them an immediate audience and insisted they stay in the palace. He also lavished gifts on them, and when Caspar explained away their injuries by claiming they'd been acquired during a robbery, he expressed his indignation at bandits daring to set about three such eminent guests in his kingdom, and reimbursed them.

"And he's so interested in our quest to find the prince," Melchior said, admiring his new hair cut in the tiny pocket mirror. "I only wish I was able to tell him more."

"If I'd realised how little you knew about it, I'd never have agreed to accompany you!" said Caspar, "but on the other hand, I've made some good contacts and I've given out most of my business card papyri."

"And," said Balthazar, "he seems to think we might find the prince in Bethlehem. That should save us a lot of time. Caspar's idea of checking each town in alphabetical order, would have taken months."

"I've already told you, the star will guide us," said Melchior.

"Well, just in case it doesn't, Herod's given us some new maps and when we've finished visiting the prince in Bethlehem, he's promised us a big welcome on our way home."

With Herod's maps, it had been fairly straightforward to find Bethlehem. But disappointingly, there was no palace.

And the star seemed to shine directly over the whole town without specifically indicating any particular dwelling.

"I told you a star was no good as a navigational tool," said Balthazar, "but you wouldn't listen! Now what're we going to do?"

"Well, we could knock on every door and ask," suggested Caspar, "and at the same time, I have some business flyers I could deliver..."

In the end, it had been Wing Lee who discovered the location of the child they'd come to see. He'd asked the women who were drawing water at the well and discovered the most suitable candidate had been born in a stable and was currently living there with his parents on the far side of Bethlehem.

"Nonsense!" said Melchior and for once, the others agreed with him.

Three days later, after knocking on door after door, asking about newly-born babies, it appeared that against all odds, Wing Lee had been correct.

It was no wonder the poor woman clutched the baby to her chest and the man put his arm protectively around them both, as Melchior, Caspar and Balthazar entered the stable, thought Wing Lee. With their colourful, costly robes and jewelled turbans, they appeared to be very foreign... and very intimidating.

Melchior bowed deeply, "My friends and I have travelled many miles to pay homage to your son and to bring you many gifts—"

"A *few* gifts," corrected Caspar.

Very few, thought Wing Lee. There was hardly anything left in the ornate chest he was holding. When they'd set out, there had been four such trunks. Thank goodness they'd arrived in Bethlehem before all the gifts had been sold.

The man and woman glanced at each other nervously and seemed afraid to move.

Melchior bowed again, "May I present you with…"

Wing Lee reached inside the chest and withdrew a small box. "Gold," he whispered to Melchior and passed it to him.

"Gold," said Melchior proudly and laid the box at the woman's feet.

Caspar elbowed Melchior out of the way, "And may I present you with…"

Wing Lee handed him an elaborate bottle. "Frankincense," he whispered.

"My business card papyrus," said Caspar, holding one out, "and Frankincense oil." He placed them next to the gold.

"Frankincense oil is very good for the skin," said Melchior, "and for combatting stress."

Balthazar pushed between the two wise men and flung his arms wide. "And may I present you with…"

Wing Lee took a box out of the chest and opened it. He closed it and put it back.

"What was that, Wing Lee?" Balthazar said out of the corner of his mouth.

"It's not suitable for a child, sir. It has small, sharp parts. But here," he said taking out the last item in the coffer, "is some Myrrh oil."

Balthazar announced his gift and placed the bottle next to the Frankincense.

"Excellent for reducing wrinkles," said Melchior.

"I wouldn't say they looked overjoyed," said Melchior on their way back to the tent.

"I would think, sir, they were rather overwhelmed by your spectacular presence," said Wing Lee.

"Yes, yes, I suppose so… But it was very disappointing, nonetheless. I'd expected rapturous thanks at least… Is anyone else feeling a little deflated now our mission is over?"

"It's not completely over, don't forget, we've been invited to stay with King Herod in Jerusalem," said Caspar.

Melchior brightened. "Yes, that's true. Well, I suggest we set out tomorrow. What d'you say, chaps?"

"If you don't mind, sir," said Wing Lee, "I'd prefer not to go to Jerusalem, I'd like to go straight home."

"That's very inconvenient, Wing Lee. Who will do all the work?"

"Well, sir, I expect King Herod will supply you with new slaves for your return journey."

"Yes, I suppose so."

"Wing Lee's been a good and faithful servant," said Caspar. "We should let him go."

Balthazar agreed.

"So, kind sirs, I would merely trouble you for my back-dated wages…"

"Wages? Certainly not!" said Melchior. "The nerve of the man! He leaves us in the lurch and then expects us to pay him!" The other two nodded in agreement.

Early the following morning before the sun had risen, Wing Lee packed up his masters' tent and belongings and loaded them on to the camels.

"I'm going to navigate," said Balthazar.

"Nonsense!" said Melchior, slapping his camel with a stick to urge him forward. "I got us here. We shall follow the star to get home."

"How d'you know the star's going in that direction?"

Wing Lee didn't hear the reply because it was masked by the sound of Balthazar retching. The maps which he'd been holding were forgotten as he dangled precariously over the camel's side and they fell, unseen, to the ground.

Wing Lee picked them up and dusted them down. He'd sell them when he got home and they'd cover some of his lost earnings. Sitting on a rock, he opened his pack and got out the box he'd kept back from the baby the day before.

It was totally unsuitable for a child with its delicate Chinese glass bowl, carved wooden rod, metal needle and silk thread. Much too dangerous. The silken cord was attached to the wooden bar which was balanced on the top of the bowl. The needle was tied to the other end of the silk thread and it dangled and spun freely. Wing Lee watched and eventually, the needle stopped moving and simply hung, pointing at the large letter N which was painted on the box. The other end of the needle pointed to a letter S and on the right was E and the left, was W.

"So," said Wing Lee out loud, "the needle is pointing north to Jerusalem but I need to go east." He consulted the map and then packed everything away. He would travel east and if he hurried, he'd be home in a few months.

He wondered how long it would take his masters to follow the star to Jerusalem.

Quite a long time, he thought, since the star they were following seemed to be taking them due south.

About the author
Dawn's third book *Extraordinary* was published by Chapeltown in October 2017. She has had four other books published as well as stories in various anthologies, including horror and speculative fiction. Two of her books are historical romances and there are several more coming in 2020. Dawn has written two plays to commemorate the First World War, one of which has been performed in England, Germany and France.

www.dawnknox.com

Like a Lamb...

Linda Flynn

"Take care Maria!" My mother's voice echoed down the road. Not that I was really listening. *What does it even mean?* I wondered as I lurched towards a seat at the back of a bus and fell into it. *Do the drivers get extra points for the number of passengers they topple over?*

There wasn't much for me to do on the number 333 as it rattled through pools of light, before clattering around dark corners, so I snatched up a newspaper that was draped across the back seat. I flicked through the pages filled with the same old stories, using the same words: countries fighting, continents uniting, power struggles between nations, agreements shattered, allegiances broken. And the same for the people in the paper.

I thumbed through to the horoscopes. At the top of the page it said, 'Follow your stars'. So I did.

Then I realised that there are lots of stars, a sky full, so how do I know which one to follow?

The first three comets I chased burned themselves out rather quickly, but I gained greater wisdom about men, particularly the spiritual, venerable and estimable.

Even now, I can't smell the scent of myrrh without thinking about Melchior. At first I was impressed by his gravitas, his neatly pressed charcoal suit and the gleaming black limo that he drove around in. Turned out that he was an undertaker and the gloomy face was his normal expression.

Now I don't know if you've ever become besotted by a priest, but let me tell you, it's fairly pointless. For one thing, Father Balthasar never noticed me as he had his eyes raised to heaven and for another it got quite chilly hanging around old churches whilst he wafted his frankincense about. Anyway, I learned my scriptures well.

The next seemed quite hopeful at first, an investment banker. Even I knew that I had gone from one extreme to another. Gaspar showered me with trinkets, (that he sent his secretary out to buy,) but not his time. I could only take so much jewellery, so in the end I pawned the gold and went travelling.

Whilst hitching a ride on a donkey cart I met Joe, a carpenter and a cabinet maker. *That's useful,* I thought, *a man who is good with his hands.*

We muddled along okay, although he used to sit bolt upright at night, disturbed by vivid dreams.

Then we had The Conversation. It seemed that we both had things on our mind. He shuffled in his seat in that shifty way that men sometimes get. Turned out that he had got behind on his tax returns and so he would have to travel to Jerusalem to sort it out, at the busiest time of year too.

Then it was my turn, so I told him that two of us would be joining him, as I was expecting a baby. He didn't exactly jump on his chair with joy, but that was probably just as well, as it was one that he'd made himself.

It was a somewhat bumpy journey in the donkey cart, so you can imagine my consternation when we finally arrived and he admitted that he hadn't booked ahead. The streets were thronging with people, so of course there was no accommodation left, not even an Airbnb.

So there I was, about to give birth in a in a manky outbuilding in a busy town. *That's typical,* I thought, *I am engaged to an impoverished furniture restorer and staying somewhere without so much as a stick of furniture.*

No sooner had we settled in, than my contractions started. As if that wasn't bad enough, we were both shaken by a great flash of blinding light, the walls shook and rubble flew against the building.

"That's it!" I yelled above the noise. "As soon as this baby's born we're out a here! We're not waiting around for a bomb to fall on us. Herod's men have killed enough babies and children already!"

Joe nodded and softly added, "We'll make our way to Egypt."

With all the chaos going on around us, I didn't want to risk going to the hospital. There could not have been a worse time to give birth.

Luckily my baby was born very quickly, but oh my word, I don't want to go through that again in a hurry! Even the shepherds in the neighbouring field came scurrying down to check that I was okay, like I needed an audience. Anyway, they told me that they knew how to help, having birthed numerous sheep in the fields, so I guess for them it was just one more lamb.

I sent WhatsApp photos of my beautiful baby boy to my family, friends, exes and all those people who had forgotten about me, before sleeping, utterly exhausted.

The following morning Joe leapt up to a banging on the door. There were three Next Day Signed For deliveries. Luckily he got there before they tried to shove a "We tried to deliver" card through the letter box.

My baby boy blinked open his eyes as we unwrapped the three gifts in front of him: gold from Gaspar, Frankincense from Balthasar and myrrh from Melchior.

I leant over and tucked the blankets around him, protecting his soft skin. His little mouth puckered. I stroked his rounded cheek and allowed his tiny hand to clasp my finger. He lit up my world. As I pulled him close to me I felt overwhelmed by the urge to save him from evil, danger or harm. My son, my love, my life.

About the author

Linda Flynn has had two humorous novels published: *Hate at First Bite* for 7 – 9-year-olds and *My Dad's a Drag*, for teenagers. Both won Best First Chapter in The Writers' Billboard competition.

She has six educational books with the Heinemann Fiction Project. In addition she has written for a number of newspapers and magazines, including theatre reviews and several articles on dogs.

Linda has had seventeen short stories published in the Bridge House anthologies, Chapel Town, Café Lit and from the Waterloo Festival. Her website is: www.lindaflynn.com.

Moon-mother

Elizabeth Cox

I was born to the daughter of the moon.

Marta told me that my mother was the most beautiful daughter of the moon. She was ethereal, fragile, delicate and mutable. I didn't know what that word meant when I was younger, although I have since learned it means to be inconstant, changeable, like the watery clouds which wraith the moon. But Marta was biased, because my mother was also her daughter, so that made her the moon didn't it? She did not speak about my father, but her faced clouded over with darkness. That I was created from the union of two people, she did not deny, but neither did she acknowledge it.

Marta is my grandmother.

Marta must have been there at my beginning, because she knew the facts. She said I emerged from my mother, like a butterfly from a chrysalis: damp and folded. My black hair was plastered against my head, my face red and crumpled. I had yelled at the top of my infant voice, but my mother was silent. Of my moon-mother, she told me very little. Of my earth-father even less.

My first steps were taken holding my grandmother's gnarled fingers with my grandfather watching. I stumbled around her flag-stoned kitchen floor clutching onto the scrubbed wooden table, where we ate most days. My grandfather would catch me when I fell, picking me up, so I could begin again. He would take me on his knee and sing soft songs to me. When I was tired, I fell asleep huddled into his plaid shirt.

There were no photographs of my mother. I would look at the polished mahogany sideboard and see pictures in silver frames reflected there. There was a large formal portrait of a young grandma and grandad, she in a beautiful white dress with pearls around her neck, him in an uncomfortable starched collar with his arm along the back of the plush chair where she was sitting. A bouquet of lilies was draped across her knee trying to hide the fact her dress was too tight across her stomach. A stray blossom had come loose and was threatening to slide to the floor from her lap. Next to that was a photo of my aunty Bridget. Although in the picture she was only a child, I could recognise her dark angry eyes. On the other side of the wedding picture, was my uncle Brian. His familiar grin radiated warmth from the black and white flatness of his portrait. But no upside-down photographs of my mutable mother were reflected in that shiny wooden surface.

One rainy Saturday afternoon, when I was alone with Grandad, I could hold my tongue no longer. I looked up from the tabbed hearthrug, where I was playing, gripped the red and black tabs between my fingers and asked about her.

"Grandad," I wheedled, "tell me about my mother. What was her name?" His face blanched under his grey moustache, and his normally sparkling blue eyes were sombre. I was puzzled. Why could I not know her name?

"Nothing to say, girlie, nothing to say. Best forgotten." His voice was gruff, as he rose turning to walk towards the kitchen. "Want a cup of tea, Miriam? Or a squash? I've got chocolate biscuits if you like."

I knew then there was something secret about her existence, as chocolate biscuits were only brought out when Mrs Anderson from the Mother's Union visited my grandma.

"Squash thanks, Grandad – lemon please." I sat in his stuffed armchair and dangled my legs from the seat, swinging them from side to side. The chair smelt of tobacco and the glass of whisky he used to drink each evening. It was like being cuddled by him. Grandad returned with the squash and the chocolate digestives and nothing more was said. We played Ludo and Snakes and Ladders on the scratched oak coffee table, whiling away the afternoon watching the rain lashing against the windows. I would have to ask Grandma.

Next morning, when I was smashing the top off my boiled egg, I watched Grandma making a cup of tea. After she poured herself a cup, she came to sit beside me at the table.

"Are you well, Miriam? What are you going to do today, when we return from church?" She smiled distractedly, as she stirred her cup. Grandma always had two sugars in her tea. I knew she was waiting to hear me say I was going to finish my homework, but I had other plans.

Invariably, we went to church on Sundays. It was the most boring day of the week. I had to wear my best dress *and* brush my hair *and* shake hands with the vicar who had sweaty palms. He always gripped my fingers too tightly. That ordeal came after sitting on a hard bench in a freezing church for what seemed like hours listening to his droning voice and the out of tune singing from the choir and congregation. The lily pollen brought on fits of sneezing.

"Nothing much, Grandma," I replied, "I think I'll look for my mother after lunch." Grandma nearly choked on her cuppa. "Do you know where I should start?"

"I'll hear no more of that!" She thumped the table making the tea slop all over the tablecloth. "Go and get yourself ready for church." She whipped the boiled egg from under my nose. I tried to grab it, as there was still a morsel of yolk in the bottom which I had left until last, but to no avail. The shell was consigned to the bin and the egg cup into the washing up bowl. I stalked off up to my

110

bedroom pulling faces at Grandma behind her back. I really wanted that egg. My tummy was going to rumble all through church.

Shrugging into my navy woollen coat which itched like mad around the neck and yanking up my white socks, I was more determined than ever now to look for my mother. Perhaps I should ask the vicar; he knew most things. I'd have to put up with his slimy handshake, but it would be worth it.

I followed one step behind Grandma and Grandpa into the church. As we took our seats on the usual pew, I grinned at my best friend Sally who was sitting opposite. Perhaps she would help me in my search later. We could start whilst the grownups were gossiping in the churchyard.

After the service was over, we filed through the stone porch out into the blinding sunshine. The vicar was standing there dispensing blessings and creepy handshakes. When it was my turn, I walked straight up to him and grabbed his hand. He did have the grace to look shocked.

"Good sermon, Vicar," I said in my poshest voice mimicking the words I had heard Sally's mum say. He was taken aback.

"Thank you, Miriam, I'm glad you enjoyed it," he replied spit flying from his lips.

"Vicar, do you know where my mother is? I'm trying to find her." I gazed up at him, my eyes wide.

"Why no, Miriam, I did not know your mother. You must ask your grandmother." Colour crept up his face, until it was puce. He swiftly moved to shake hands with the next person who was emerging from the church door. He was not going to be any good then, I'd have to try somewhere else.

Undeterred, I turned to find Sally who was also making her escape from her parents.

"Come on Sal, let's go." Sally followed me, until we were around the back of the church where the old gravestones were. The sun heated the granite top and soft green-grey lichen provided our cushion, as we hoisted ourselves up onto the grave of a Mrs Rose Althorp who died in 1848. We didn't think she'd mind. She'd probably had granddaughters like us.

"It's like this, Sal," I began. "I need to find my mother; will you help me?"

"Course I will, Mim," she replied, poking at an earwig who had decided to cross her path. "Where do you want to start?"

"Well I thought we'd look around here first; she may have a gravestone if she's dead."

"True, but there are lots of gravestones. Do we have to read them all?" Sally was now distracted by a butterfly which had landed on the plastic flowers in the pot at the head of the grave.

"Well we could start with the newer ones, because she was alive when I was born eleven years ago."

Sally looked at me in awe, admiring my logic.

"OK then," she replied sliding down off the warm stone.

I joined her, and we skipped round to the newer graves at the side of the graveyard hidden under the arms of a spreading Yew tree.

"Where shall we start?" she whispered, swinging around a Yew branch. "I'm scared we might know some of the people here. It's creepy. What's her name?"

I had realised then that I could not look for someone whose name I did not know.

"No, you're right it's creepy here. Let's go," I said. "We can look another day. I can hear Grandma calling me."

"Whatever!" Sally shrugged, and together we raced

across the grass to the gravel path where our families were waiting for us.

"Where've you been?" Grandma scolded. "We're waiting to go home. The roast'll be burned."

I wrinkled up my nose at the thought of the overdone roast beef. "Just looking for my mother," I announced.

She stared at me for a moment, then said, "I'll have no more of that nonsense, Miriam." She scowled and grabbed hold of my arm steering me out through the lych-gate and into the lane.

Fortunately, the beef was not burnt, and we sat down to Sunday dinner in silence. Throughout the meal, Grandma was preoccupied, and Grandad was trying to be cheerful. Aunty Bridget had come over for dinner, and her and Grandma were closeted in the kitchen for ages. Bridget's eyes were still angry, but she smiled at me as she helped me to brussels sprouts.

After dinner, Grandma called me into the kitchen.

"Come and help me, Miriam, there's a good girl."

I was puzzled but mildly pleased. She never let me help with the Sunday washing-up saying that I was clumsy and a threat to her best china. Nevertheless, I got up meekly from my chair following her into the room, where dirty pots and pans were spread over the table.

"Sit down here, Miriam," she said patting the old horsehair-stuffed chair opposite her at the table.

"But Grandma, I thought I was supposed to be helping you with the dishes!"

"All in good time, sweetheart, I need to talk to you for a moment." She placed her chapped hand over mine and squeezed gently. "I know you want to find your mother."

"Oh, Grandma, where shall I start? Do you know where she is? What's her name?" Words were tumbling out of my mouth in rapid succession, tripping over each other in the rush to be heard.

"I don't know where she is."

I felt the tears well up in my eyes and rapidly brushed them away.

"She left after an argument. I have never seen her since." Now it was Grandma's time to become tearful, although her face was cold. "She returned home in desperation to give birth to you but would not stay. I was too stubborn, too full of my own pride to stop her leaving with that man." She spat the word 'man'. "We could not save her. She left you with us to be cared for. You were a gift to us."

"But Grandma, what was her name? What colour hair did she have, what colour eyes? Do I look like her?" My heart was full of questions.

This was when she told me my mother was a daughter of the moon.

"Her name was Diana. She had silver-blonde hair and pale green eyes flecked with brown. You look nothing like her, except for your eyes." She spoke softly, her gaze distant; remembering.

"Why wouldn't you tell me before?" I was getting angry. "I wanted to know. I asked you so many times!"

"I'm sorry, child, but I was hurt too. It was easier to forget about her, pretend she never existed. Except every time I looked into your eyes, I knew she was there,"

It was my turn to lay my hand over Marta's and squeeze it tight. I watched, as hot angry tears spilled from her wrinkled eyelids down her cheeks then dripped onto her best cardigan making the wool damp. In that moment, I knew I had grown up and found my mother.

"It's fine, Marta, don't worry. Would you like a nice cup of tea?" I smiled at her patting her hand. I decided I would not ask about my earth-father; not yet.

That night I lay on my bed basking in the moonlight which shone through the window panes. Never again would I draw the curtains. I had found my moon-mother, and I could spend time with her every night. I saw her rise in the sky higher each night, until she was there in her fullness. Then I watched her wane again, until she was gone anticipating her gradual return. Sometimes glowering rain clouds scudded across the sky obscuring her beams, until I wished them away, hoping to see her more clearly.

"Good night my beautiful, mutable moon-mother." I whispered each night into the darkness, before I went to sleep.

About the author

Elizabeth has appeared in three other Bridge House Anthologies: *Baubles* 2016, *Glit-er-ary* 2017 and *Crackers* 2018. She enjoys writing poetry and short stories. She is currently working on a novel set in Anglo-Saxon England. Since she has moved to a new house, she can no longer stare at the mountains when procrastinating, but watches the birds in her lovely new garden. She is currently the chair of the Bangor Cellar Writers Group in Bangor.

New Shoes for Christmas

Nicole Fitton

Pieces of his imagination capture my soul as I sleep, and I am awoken abruptly feeling its loss. He holds it to ransom. *It'll cost you more than a penny to get it back laddie* he whispers. He seals the box tight and places it on the table at the end of the bed. I can't see it clearly, but somehow I know it's there. Escape is not promised, but I'll do my best.

I can see it clearer now. Bathed in light beyond the crisp linen and white noise its shape has formed and I hold it in my mind's eye. The roadmap to my future is translucent and hollow. I know it keeps my future and at that moment I want to make it out more than anything in the world. I calculate the distant and imagine my journey all stretched and elongated, as though it's there but not there, like a 3D hologram or a ghost. I wobble not convinced I possess enough strength or courage. At times everything is in sharp focus, and I know what I need to do. I need to push forward, head first, arm raised like Superman and project myself towards the end of the bed. But just when I think I've got the hang of things, just when I'm starting to make progress, I'm pulled back tighter than a big dog on a short leash. The keeper of my soul has waged war against me, and it's up to me to fight back in this game of life.

Stretched sheets bind my feet. My skin is sealed within a cotton shell. A bedtime tortilla with a live filling. My arms try to lengthen, and I dig my small nails into the Egyptian cotton. I am hanging on but only just. For a moment I lose sight of him, and my eyes flicker. *Now then big man, ya did nay think I'd leave ya did ye?* I try to shake my head, but only my mind moves. I am moving towards the end of the bed now, voices around me chime and chirp. It's a lesson in forced fun as no one is sure if I'll survive the night. But tonight, my eyes will be out on storks, lollipops from Willy Wonka's chocolate factory, I will not drift off to the land of Nod, but I will survive. I know I will always be my brother's keeper.

A week overdue was not part of her birthing plan; there was no column for plan B. She was as prepared as a pastor's wife needed to be. Martha had thought of classical music and birthing pools; of candles and soft scents. Her husband called on all that was holy, and a prayer chain the length of Britain mobilised. But fourteen days in and the good Lord had turned a deaf ear – babies? What babies, I don't know about any babies.

Bean bags were replaced with stirrups and hot curries with gas and air. Any notions she still held of a natural delivery withered and her dreams exited as day fifteen dawned. Pastor Pete proclaimed a message of hope, and she throws up all over his brogues. Contractions refused to come, and shoeless Pete knelt at every given moment. Martha would bargain with the devil if it meant she could fit back into normal knickers again.

Complications they said as they wheeled in the incubators and placed them at the end of the bed. Martha felt small and vulnerable. Dull rhythmic sounds pulsed and pinged. A circle of mechanical prayer surrounded her – each wire a voice, each light a beacon.

"We'll take it from here, Pastor," they said as Pete was shouldered gently from the room. Secretly she was relieved. A chorus of artificial heartbeats peeled around the room and the bright white lights focussed in at the business end. Martha thought of fairy lights and Christmas carols. She had a mind to sing and wondered if it would be appropriate.

'Hark The Herald Angels Sing' was her go-to favourite and she beat out time with the back of her wedding ring on the steel-framed bed.

"It's started to snow, Martha, it'll be the first white Christmas in over twenty years," said the midwife. Her name badge read 'Mary' – the irony was not lost. In her drug-fuelled state, Martha strained a smile. Picking up her fallen face from the floor she tried to stick bits of it back together. But she was numb, and the words wouldn't form. When all this was over, she would make the most of the free dental appointments she told herself.

There was no clock that she could see, but if she had to guess she would have said she'd been there for all eternity waiting for the world to form within her. She pushed and sweated and almost gave up, but a promise was a promise.

Where there were two, now lay one. A puff of air between life and death was all that separated them, and she prayed and cursed in equal measure. Pete returned, his face held ash where once was flame. He had been and addressed one nativity, proclaiming the saviours' birth while she delivered the other. Now he was here, standing tall in his shiny new Christmas shoes.

Pete rolled the cot with its frosted plastic viewing window and lengths of cables towards her, and she peered in at the small bundle wrapped tightly in cotton.

Only time would tell if history would be repeated, or if somewhere at the edge of time where the fabric was fraying, a new world would start to rise. Pete caught Martha's hand and rested it on top of the domed cover.

"We need to give him a name, Martha," he said, his words landing soft and full of feathers.

Martha nodded. In the hours which passed, she watched from the outside as tasks were completed and tests were taken. Her son, her first born, screamed like a banshee at the end of her bed, eyes wide as if the world was already painful and familiar.

"His name is Cain," she said.

About the author:
Nicole Fitton is a freelance writer who has lived in such glamorous locations as London, New York, and Croydon! She currently lives in Devon with her family. Her career has spanned three decades working in PR and marketing within Europe and the USA. She currently works within healthcare management in the UK. She is a lover of words and writes both short and long stories. Many of her short stories have been short and longlisted and she hopes one day to be the bride and not always the bridesmaid!

www.nicolefittonauthor.com

Roses are Red

Aqsa Mustafa

Some say bullet wounds hurt, some say paper cuts are the worst. But no one talks about the pain caused by something as small as breathing in the wrong perfume.

I'm outside the upstairs spare bedroom, the room we had been renovating for our little girl. There is a crib in the corner all set up, books on the shelves we thought we could read to a newborn (we were over-excited parents, one could say), and a giant owl rug on the floor. There are pink curtains on the two bow windows overlooking the street, our attempt at tipping a hat to her gender, along with an assortment of dolls and stuffed animals lined on the sills.

Everything is covered in a thin film of dust. I haven't crossed this threshold since the day we came home from the hospital with the baby bag over Zach's shoulder but no baby in my arms or belly. I come here every day, come to see if maybe what I think has happened is actually a horrible dream and my princess is safe in her room, fast asleep and dreaming of bunnies. But she isn't here. She never is. Today, once again, the crib remains empty.

Zach came home late last night, his midnight hair rumpled and a strange perfume wafting from his shirt. I didn't say a word as he traipsed around the half-lit room, changing into pyjamas and avoiding my eyes. He knew I was awake, watching him.

The baby took something away with her that day at the hospital, from both of us. When they brought her to me for that one time and I held her in my arms, I poured my soul into that little figure, trying to will it into animation. But the paper-thin lids did not open, the tiny bird chest did not flutter with life, the rosebud lips did not part to release a twisted wail. I didn't cry either, just looked at her. And when they took her away, I forgot to ask for my heart back.

Zach and I had been so much in love. I remember those days as if through a fog, as if my mind connects with the fabric of that past only reluctantly, knowing if I delve too far I couldn't find my way out of the illusion and back into reality. Our love had been bright and flashy, full of intimate gestures and strong promises that left people staring with awe. My mother once told me, "Bright things are often brittle on the inside."

But the intensity of our love hadn't been at fault, no. It was just *her*, the idea of her, the dream of her… she had been ripped from our lives as suddenly and as finally as a circus artist pulls a tablecloth from under the dishes, leaving us clattering like cheap china. The glasses and plates eventually settle down, albeit now on the less glamorous table surface, and just like that we had settled to, into a life of perpetual silence and shifty glances that tried to measure the other from the corner of the eye, struggling to figure out what was going on in the other head. But where before there had been an almost telepathic connection, now there existed only stillness and a ringing hush.

Today, after assuring myself that no down-headed cherub lay amongst the congeries of stuffed animals and velvet pillows in the crib, I stare at the room as if it held a great secret I was only a random thought away from unravelling. Weak sunlight filters through the heavy curtains – curtains that haven't been opened since that summer Monday. Rain drums against the glass outside, the patter in sync with my speeding heartbeat.

Today, Zach's foreign perfume still strong in my nose, his fleeting kiss still heavy on my lips as he left for the day, and his beseeching stare still imprinted on my bowed forehead – waiting, hoping, despairing – I step into the room.

Jasmine Rose Holland. That's what we would have named her. A heavy name for something so tiny, I now think, wishing we hadn't promised Zach's mother. That old woman, with her supercilious air of judgment, meant well, but I should have taken a hint from the fact that the smallest kitten in her cat's recent litter is named Theodore.

I would have called her just Rose. Rose for the blush on her cheeks, for the tiny heart-like mouth, for the warm, twinkling eyes I knew she would have, eyes hiding beneath transparent lids heavy with Zach's lashes.

I am by the crib, running a finger over the lacquered guardrail and coming away with a thin coating of dust. She would have had a glowing smile and a bubbling laugh. Like a carbonated drink shaken in the bottle and the cap twisted open, her laugh would overflow, the waves of it touching every person in the room till they couldn't help looking at each other, a little flustered but laughing back nonetheless. They would not be able to help laughing back.

I can see her in the crib now, lying with her arms bent at right angles by her head and her feet kicking off the duvet. Her baby cap has slipped over the little bumpy head. Her chest rises and falls, breathe rattling like a motor engine trying to start.

I smile, reach forward, and adjust the cap.

When her eyes open, I cannot say it shocked me. I'm her mother; of course she would react to my touch. Babies know their mothers merely by smell, and I am right here by her, leaning over and touching her face. It is only natural that she should wake.

"Hello, Pumpkin," I say, running a finger down her powder-soft cheek. The skin is still flushed from birth, covered with a smattering of pale dots.

She wriggles under the sheets, lips moving and big eyes roving over my face. I laugh.

"Are you hungry, love?" I ask. "Is that what it is? Are you hungry?" My breasts are aching already, full to bursting with milk.

Gently, careful of the floppy head, I slide my hands under her and lift the feather-light weight toward my chest, blankets and all. So small, so insubstantial. If not for the tiny head peeking through the folds of felt, I would think there was nothing but cloth in my arms.

Rocking her though she does not utter a single cry, does not gurgle deep in her throat as she works her mouth searching for a nipple, I find my way to the chair in the corner and settle gingerly onto it. Then I open my collar and pull one full breast out.

Her head is in the crock of my elbow. I lift it up, toward the dark nipple that already has a drop of white hanging precariously off it, but she doesn't take it into her mouth. Though I try and try, nestling her mouth against the hard, throbbing spot, she does not suck. Tears spring into my eyes.

"Rose, darling," I coo, fisting my exposed breast to relieve some of the building tension inside. My hand comes away wet. "Please, drink, Rose. You have to drink, love, if you are to thrive. Don't you want to grow up? Grow big and strong and tall, just like daddy? Of course, you want that. You must drink."

But she wouldn't take the tit, no. She only looks at me, never blinking, eyes too big for her face.

"Rose, please…" I beg, voice breaking. My heart is like a stone in my chest, a dead thing inside a dead thing. I rock her head and wish I could rip my skin out and lay all the pain on the floor. That way I could sift through the mess and see all the different forms of torment one human body can hold enclosed inside meat and bones. I can feel my soul on my lips, a trapped being trying to force its way out of my blood and fly free. I want it to fly. I want it to take the pain away. "Oh, Rose…"

"Anna?"

I lift my head and there is Zach, framed in the doorjamb with a hand on the knob and an unreadable expression on his face. A vein is throbbing on his temple and he holds his jaws clamped so tight I wonder how my name fought through the bars of those teeth.

"Zach," I say. "Zach, Rose won't drink!" I hold up the blankets. "Look at her. She just won't drink my milk!"

He closes his eyes and rubs the bridge of his nose. His hands are shaking. A bright red flush rises from his collar and surges to his temple. "Ann, don't do this, *please…*" His words tremble too, as if they are being wrenched out of his body with a force beyond the constraints of human will power.

"But—"

He is by my side in an instant, ripping the blankets out of my hands and throwing them back in the crib. I scream and start after them, but he grabs my arms and holds fast.

"No!" he says, red-veined eyes boring into mine. A tear blooms under the right pupil before going over the edge and tumbling down his cheek. "No, you will stay here and you will listen to me. She's gone, Anna!" he yells, shaking me. "She's gone, and I want you to stop doing this!"

"Let me go, Zach," I say through a gasp. "Let me go. My baby—"

"—is dead!"

Those emphatic words make me stop and stare. It is as if I am seeing the scene from outside, from an impersonal vantage point that has nothing to do with the body Zach now presses against his chest in a crushing grip.

"Our girl's dead, Anna," he says again. His voice is harsh as he pushes a hand around the nape of my neck and cradles my head, cradles it like I'd never gotten to cradle my Rose. "Come back to me, Anna. Please come back to me," he begs. "You are *killing* me!"

"She was right here," I whisper, pulling away from his grip just enough to look down at my hands, at the forlorn breast still hanging from my collar. My hands are dry, the breast once more small and insubstantial.

He is crying now, shoulders shaking with the force of compressed emotions finally finding a way out of burning body and soul. His knees buckle and we slide to the floor. I rub a hand over his rumpled hair.

"What was it about, Zach?" I ask. I am not crying like he is. My eyes, like the rest of my being, are two dried husks too tired to produce tears. "That fight. Do you remember? I can't remember."

He buries his face in my shoulder, fingers pulling at the roots of my hair. The way he is grabbing at me reminded me of a vine wrapped around a post, that support the only thing keeping it from tumbling to the ground and being trampled into oblivion. "I am *so* s-sorry," he weeps, voice muffled in my hair.

"There is no need to be a spoiled bitch, Anna!"

That's what he'd yelled at me that day as we stood in the middle of our room getting in each other's faces. I cannot remember what we had disagreed on. It might have been the renovation plans, it might have been his mother meddling with our lives again, it might even have been a wet towel left over the staircase railing. But what it had ended in was *this*.

We were both calling each other names, but those words of his, those *specific* words, for some reason shot through me like a bullet. Looking at his bloodshot eyes and heightened colour, smelling his anger and sweat, suddenly I couldn't breathe.

I had rushed out of the room, afraid one of us might say something far worse than name calling. Perhaps it was the stress of the baby, perhaps it was just us, but our fights were getting more and more frequent those past couple months and I didn't want that to be the last thing in our relationship. As I stepped to the head of the stairs and grabbed the railing, my knees were knocking into each other with the force of bottled-up emotions. Perhaps that's what made my foot slip.

I cannot remember what happened after that. All that's substantial in my memory of the next few seconds is a back-bending pain in my abdomen. There were other pains too, but that was the one that I remember explicitly. *My baby.*

Zach had come running, only to find me with half my body up the stairs and the rest lying spread on the living room floor covered in my own blood and birthing fluids.

The doctors had tried to save the baby, even assuring Zach enough for him to bring the prepared baby bag over and wait in the lobby for half a day, but it was no use. Rose didn't want to stay, and she hadn't.

"I wish I could change it, Anna," Zach said now. "I wish I could bring her back. You know I would give my life to bring her back." Strains of deep compunction and unrelieved remorse were like fate's threads in his voice, heavy with the burden of his smote conscience. He, like me, couldn't stop wondering what could have been. What if we hadn't fought? What if we had been like the couples on TV where pregnancy is all about love and care? What if we had realized what was more important?

Zach is shuddering in my arms, like a machine having spent its fuels stalls through the last stages of its life, and I find myself stroking his heavy curls yet again as I say, "It's alright. It's alright now. Everything is fine," as if it was he who had conjured a child out of thin air and tried to feed it. Then again, maybe he did similar things, just that I'd never caught him like he had walked onto me.

I could see clearly now, see what I was about to throw

away with my own hands. We could live in the past as much as we liked but all it would ever do was drag us down into a never-ending abyss of shattered dreams and hopes. There was nothing to be accomplished from it, nothing to be gained.

Zach lifts his head from my shoulder and holds my gaze. A tender, tremulous brush of his knuckles against my cheek is all it takes for the tears concealed behind dry, wide eyes to spill over my lashes. I draw a shattered breath as he captures my chin between his thumb and forefinger.

Privation of the hollow burn in my stomach, rising from the feeling that I was truly alone in this hell, has left me curiously light. I am ready to float away, Zach's touch the only thing keeping me grounded. Why did I think I was alone, when he had lost as much as I had? Why did I doubt him, when he was the only person who could feel what I felt, who could boast of understanding even a mere semblance of the pain that smouldered in the pit of my stomach like acid? In my blind ignorance, I thought a mother lost more when her child was gone, forgetting that the father didn't even have the consolation of remembering the baby as a part of his body.

I look at the crib. Tomorrow, I will throw it away. Or tomorrow I will pack it and carry it to the attic, forgetting about it till another time.

A corner of the sheets is visible through the railings and I can see my own terrible attempts at embroidery stand out on the snow-white linen. I am a tyro hand with the needles, more likely to stab my own poor thumb than succeed in making a smooth stitch.

"Remember when I tried to embroider?" I suddenly ask.

His brow furrows, but he turns his head and follows my gaze, finds the sheets and barks out a short laugh. "A horse," he says, voice still wobbly. "That's a horse."

It isn't. It's a pigeon, but he can be forgiven for the snipe considering the distinctly equine beak, cylindrical body, and thin stick legs longer than the bird's torso.

I push at his shoulder. "You bought a *transformer* for her!" I remind him, in case he had forgotten.

"I thought she would like it!"

"A transformer for a newborn, Zach! *Really?*"

"Well, you wanted to read *The Mayor of Casterbridge* to her," he accuses. "Don't think I didn't see you hiding that damned book behind the fairytales." He points to the right edge of the shelves, where a dark corner of said volume was just visible. "Right there."

"It's educational!" I say.

We're both laughing now, leaning against each other, in our daughter's room. And for the first time in months, I feel at peace. For the first time, I feel like there is a chance of moving on, of building our life back. And when Zach kisses my cheek and whispers "I'm sorry," again, I know he means the foreign perfume on his shirt, but I am still ready to forgive. He had lost me for a moment and, while I gave myself up to my demons, he tried to fight his in other ways. It's now time to heal. The demons, still lurking in the shadows, are beaten back for now.

"Bright things are often brittle," my mother once said. As I look at Zach wiping the snot from under his nose with the edge of my sleeve, I realize she had forgotten that the sun was bright too, and I don't think it's brittle.

About the author
Aqsa Mustafa is a Pakistani storyteller who has found it easier to talk to blank papers and computer screens than to people. She aims at bringing all the mermaids and boggarts living in her head to life so that other children can play with them and realize that dreams don't necessarily have to be forgotten in the morning.

Sharing Mary

Alyson Faye

Jemma kicked over her chair, grabbed her smartphone and stormed out of *'Café Calm'*. The rest of the yoga class watched her departure in varying states ranging from amusement to bemusement.

"What's her problem?" asked a newbie to the group.

A few of the others arched their eyebrows and smirked in an all-knowing way. Their leader Angie Hawkins enlightened her. "The cast list for this year's Nativity play at the local church has been posted this morning. Jemma's daughter didn't get Mary or the Angel Gabrielle."

The other yummy mummies shook their blonde tresses in fake sympathy.

"I'm afraid Jemma's girl is the back end of the donkey this year. It's the glasses you see. She's just started wearing them and well…"

Everyone sighed in motherly understanding mode. "Obviously, Mary can't be performed by a girl in glasses. It doesn't fit the scenario, does it? No opticians in Bethlehem." (A few of the group sniggered). "And my Ellie has the most beautiful blue eyes." Angie's acolytes all nodded their glossy ponytails in agreement.

The newbie kept her opinions to herself. She understood only too well this was the price of entry into this particular club.

At home in her space-age kitchen Jemma banged cupboard doors, tossed some Monsoon cushions around and practised deep breathing. The cat eyed her incuriously from his perch next to the tropical aquarium, where he hovered 23 hours out of 24 a day.

"It's so damn unfair. It's not about talent or voice projection, it's all about who donates the most funds."

She glared at the cast list pix on her smartphone. At the top was Angie's daughter, Ellie, as Mary and her younger sibling who'd grabbed the role of the Angel Gabrielle. "Nothing to do with their Dad donating a percentage of his building firm's profits to the renovation of the church roof," muttered Jemma darkly.

To her chagrin even the divorcing neighbours, whose noisy fights entertained the cul-de-sac every Saturday night, could take parental pride in their twins playing two of the Three Kings.

"Shouldn't divorce mean your children can't even be in the Nativity?" Jemma wondered aloud to Herbie the cat, whilst she absent-mindedly pushed him off his fish hunting perch. "What's the point of being in a stable long-term marriage, if the local vicar doesn't reward your children?"

The Reverend Trevor Tempest had been, in his first incarnation, a bit part actor and voice-over artist. However on finding the pay too spasmodic, he'd turned, at the ripe age of forty, to the new role of Vicar which also involved costumes, props and voice projection. He directed the annual Oakworth Nativity play with great verve and style, inverting the tropes and gender-bending the roles. It was the 'must be seen at' event of the year.

Jemma's smartphone bleeped. A message appeared – *Soz hun. Just seen it. Roz :(*

Jemma hovered over the reply button – what could she say to minimise the fall out and the pain?

This was a PR nightmare. Everyone in her yoga, spin and bums and tums classes knew how vigorously she'd canvassed and pushed for Lucy to get at least a speaking part. Maybe one of the trio of singing female shepherdesses?

:) All fine. So excited for Lucy. She's a team player. Jemma hit send, with a trembling painted talon, the tip of which had been nibbled away.

After school, in the sanctuary of home, Lucy burst into tears. "No way am I playing a donkey's bum, Mum," she wailed.

"I know, darling, but you have to put a brave face on it." She soothed her daughter's wayward curls, removing her new spectacles from her damp cheeks.

"Are you mad? No one's going to see my face," Lucy's wails intensified.

The next few weeks were very stressful for Jemma, maintaining her polished façade at her classes, smiling through the rehearsals as she watched Angie Hawkins' Ellie flit and float about the stage draped in blue velvet curtains, beaming beatifically at the doll that was standing in for baby Jesus and clinging to Joseph's arm who happened to be acted by her crush, a chisel-jawed boy in the year above her. He was not quite so keen on Ellie grabbing his arm, shoulder or knee at every opportunity and often there were a few tussles between the two leads as the lad tried to free his limbs and Ellie wouldn't let go. Eventually the Vicar had to intervene with some directorial advice about Mary being her own person and inhabiting her own space. Ellie sulked for the rest of the rehearsal.

For Jemma, watching her darling girl stomp on and off the stage, bent double holding the waist of the girl playing the donkey's head, it was gut-churning.

To make it worse the Angel Gabrielle had a song specially written for her by the Vicar's song writing buddy, which she belted out centre stage holding the mic like a lollipop, whilst effectively obscuring her older sister from the audience's sight line.

"How's it going?" Angie Hawkins whispered as she slid into the seat beside Jemma, a Costa latte take out gripped in her skinny toned fingers.

"Fab," trilled Jemma, her voice going up as it always

did at times like this. "Totally marvellous. They're all so creative and talented. Every one of those children up there is a star."

"Of course they are, darling." There was a loaded pause and Jemma held her breath. "Though some are more visible, should we say, than others?"

At that moment Jemma hated her yoga and spin cycle classmate. Pure vitriol flowed through her veins.

"Darlings!" The Reverend Tempest called out. "Can you please not trample the model sheep when you're crowding around Mary. Three Kings – where are your gifts? Fetch them now. You cannot roll up to the birth of Jesus carrying a fake banana, a box of tissues and a Nike trainer. Really! What you do mean Props, that was all you could find at short notice? It's supposed to be gold, myrrh and frankincense, darling. Now Mary, could you look at baby Jesus with more love, not as though he's just puked on you."

Angie Hawkins' brow furrowed, her eyes narrowed.

Oh no, the Reverend would be for it later, thought Jemma. Though he had a point. The doll had suffered some harsh treatment through the rehearsals, being tossed to one side by Mary as soon as the curtain fell, resulting in a crack across the forehead, now hidden under the shawl.

"Can we have the donkey and the cow, please? Yes, move across to the manger, dip your heads and gaze in wonder on the baby Jesus," continued the Vicar in full creative flow.

Jemma held her breath. This was her girl's big moment. Lucy had been practising this routine for days. The donkey tap-danced over to the manger, lifted its head, braying just before the rear end collapsed into a seated position, crossing its back legs. The cow didn't budge.

Jemma's laughs pealed out, in the otherwise silent church hall.

"Right, well that's something we need to work on, I think," said the Reverend Tempest. "Let's have a drink and snack break. Back end of the donkey, perhaps I could have a teensy chat with you, please?"

"He wants me to play the donkey straight – no funny steps, no tail waggling. He's trying to subjugate my creativity, mum!" Lucy sobbed into her All White Company bedding, mascaraed eyes staring panda-like over the duvet.

Jemma gritted her teeth. This was maternal agony of a different sort. There had to be a way to resolve this. Could she arrange an accident for Angie Hawkins' girls? Push them under something? Drop something heavy on them? Though perhaps this was somewhat unkind even cruel? Or verging on criminal? There was only a few short days to go to the performance. What could happen in such a short time period? Perhaps a prayer or two wouldn't go amiss?

The day of the dress rehearsal arrived. The whole cast assembled back stage were climbing into their costumes and muttering their lines, when a screech emanated from the front of house.

The Reverend Trevor Tempest was huddled in deep and tense discussion with Angie Hawkins who was holding the arm of – Ellie, who oddly enough was not wearing her Mary costume, and odder still, was sporting a huge pair of sunglasses inside the dimly-lit church hall. Jemma slipped into the back row of seats, observing the scene with interest.

The Vicar waved his arms around. "How could you have been so irresponsible, Mrs Hawkins, as to let this happen?"

Angie's maternal hackles were well and truly up. "I resent that Vicar. This has never happened before. After all, I wear them myself and have never had a problem."

"Well you've got one now, haven't you?" The vicar riposted.

Ellie sat slumped, her golden-haired head bowed, the picture of misery.

"The G.P. said the swelling would go down in a few days so perhaps…"

"A few days!" shrieked the Reverend. "Mrs Hawkins it's the Performance tomorrow evening."

Jemma edged nearer. Curiosity mingling with a new-born sympathy. What on earth was wrong with Ellie?

"Turn up the house lights," the Vicar called out.

Ellie shrank down further into her chair. "Take off those sunglasses, Ellie sweetheart," pleaded her mother.

Jemma gazed in horror. Ellie's eyes were swollen to the size of golf balls, as well as being bloodshot. Her whole face resembled a poached turbot.

Her gasp drew Angie Hawkins attention. "It's not contagious," she swiftly said. "It's an extreme reaction to her contact lenses. She's banned from wearing them for six months. It's glasses for Ellie as of now."

Contact lenses? Jemma was non nonplussed, then the penny dropped. Of course. Ellie's gorgeous blue eyes were not as nature intended.

"I wear them too," continued Angie, "but I don't sleep in them, or 'forget' to take off my eye make-up." She glared at her teenage daughter.

Jemma looked at Ellie, shrunk to half her size and radiating teen misery. She remembered her own teenage disappointments only too well. *Poor girl.*

"I'm afraid we are going to have to go with the understudy. Of course Ellie is welcome to swap and play the part Lucy has been playing."

Realisation and humiliation registered on Angie Hawkins' tanned and botoxed face. "No Vicar, you can't mean…"

"I have a suggestion, Vicar," Jemma spoke up. Quiet

but firm. "Every child up there is a star and they all deserve their moment."

That year's Nativity was reckoned by everyone who watched it as the best they'd seen in years. Everyone agreed that Trevor Tempest had excelled himself with his creativity. His last minute idea that Mary be played by two different girls, one as a prenatal Mary and the other as a post-natal Mary, allowed the two actresses, Lucy and Ellie, to bring their own unique interpretations to the part. The innovative use of sunglasses to protect Mary's eyes from her son's heavenly glow was much admired.

Lucy and Ellie held hands at the curtain call, of which there were at least half a dozen. A personal best for Trevor Tempest. Though if you could lipread and were in the audience, you would have seen a heated exchange between the two Marys as to whose interpretation had been the most realistic.

Jemma thoroughly enjoyed the post-Nativity party – luxuriating in her role as mother of Mary and grandmother to the baby Jesus.

How divine, she thought.

About the author
Alyson lives in West Yorkshire, with her family and four rescue animals. She writes flash fiction, which has appeared on sites like the Horror Tree, zeroflash, Tubeflash, Cafe Aphra, Coffin Bell and in anthologies such as *Women in Horror Annual 2* and *DeadCades.* She has her flash fiction collection, *Badlands,* out with Chapeltown Books.

Her twitter handle is @AlysonFaye2 and she blogs at www.alysonfayewordpress.wordpress.com.

Soaring Down

Finn Clarke

I soar on the wind. I am the wind. For the first time in my life I'm not yearning but flying. Down below I can see mountain ranges, thick with trees, dotted with lakes; ridges and valleys stretching to the horizon. A glimmer of silver catches my eye.

The cage is in a clearing in the middle of a valley, grass stretching out on all sides. It is big and square, the clean metal bars evenly spaced: the door is open. I shoot upwards – a reflex not of surprise, but rejection – then recover myself and fly on. Once past I try to forget it, focusing again on the slipstreams and currents that keep me free.

The valley is one of my favourite kinds, high up in the mountains, long but not too narrow. The grass in the clearing is cropped smooth by passing deer, and the trees that spread up the mountainsides are spindly and weak; silver birch, aspen and pine giving way quickly to boulders and jagged rock. Exultation soaks back through me. To be here. Now. To have it all. I put the cage behind me, fly up to the crest of the ridge, then up again, the blue afternoon sky turning clear as I enter it: high, careless, free.

Except how can you be free when your cage awaits you? When your thoughts begin to be tied down by what's to come? I tell myself that I'm still soaring, but I know that's no longer true. The air feels different when it's your last caress; the journey's not the same. Instead of flying towards the future I am flying back to my past and it's as if the mountains know it. Now, they tell me, I am merely marking time.

But at least I still have time to mark. When I'm tired

out I stretch my wings, climb higher than usual just to prove I can, then glide back to the ridge above the valley. Settling down on its highest peak, I stare at the cage and think.

I don't need to remind myself why I'm going – I know why – but I need to prepare myself on how to be. I need to remind myself that this is a choice, however unlike one it feels, because what the giving up gets me is more important even than flying high. I need to remind myself that it is not forever. I need to remind myself that I have the key – that once inside, door closed and bolted, I will forget this, that I will be tempted to put on the chains before I'm even asked. I need to remind myself to put away my pride, my defensiveness, my criticism. I need to remind myself that these things are not my power.

It is a lot of reminding and by the time I've finished the sun has set behind me, the stars across the valley beginning to prick against the darkening sky. I shift my body, uncomfortable after so long on the hard stone. What will I lose, I wonder? Of all the opportunities I have now, all the paths leading to open doors, what will fade away through lack of use? I fear that the next time I fly the routes will be harder, that I'll have to start all over again – but with this fear comes the realisation that at least I *will* fly, that it's one fact of my future I can hold in my heart.

The thought is a rock, making me solid and stable as the mountain I sit on, and as I absorb its comfort, I realise that now is the time to go.

Standing up I stretch tall, pushing my limbs away from me as far as they will go. The sky has darkened even in those few minutes and now the moon is rising across the valley, silhouetting jagged crags against purple blue, its creamy-white face so close I feel I could go there. But no.

There is no flying to the moon tonight. Instead I take off, soar high, then plunge down towards the cage.

As I approach, I see it is no longer empty. The jailor has taken up residence, his shadow tall and forbidding behind the bars. I feel a tremor of fear, pause, then tell myself it doesn't have to be that way: most jailors are what you make them. I remember when he was just a man, when his presence was a comfort, a joy; when his absence was its own kind of cage, depriving me of the freedom to be with him. I remind myself that man is still there, his light shimmering behind the shadows; that while I may never again feel the pith of needing him, it is my job, as much as his, to help him change this latest role. I notice, as if for the first time, that he too is in the cage.

Taking courage I fly the final length, and as I come into land I see her. She is lying on the grass, sleeping, a strand of hair across her face, her mouth open, her muscles slack. I stop to watch her and as if sensing my presence she stirs, sighs, turns onto her side.

My daughter.

The surge of emotion is stronger than thought. It isn't that she's beautiful, strong, wise, special – she is all these things and more. It is that she's mine: my love, my wellspring of life... My reason for being here.

For her, I know, this isn't a cage. For her, it's a home, shelter from the storm, protection from the immensity of life. It is just the right bite-sized portion of the world for her to handle, the door hers to open as and when she sees fit; the surrounding valley a place to explore slowly and surely while a parent holds her hand. I want to be that parent. I want to be with her, for better or worse, until she no longer needs me. It is stronger than anything else.

Slowly, I walk into the cage and shut the door.

About the author

Finn Clarke's short stories have been published in magazines ranging from *Big Pulp* to *Descant* and anthologies such as Val McDermid's *Endangered Species*. Her crime novel, *Call Time*, won the CWA's 2013 Debut Dagger and she recently gained a distinction for an MA in Novel Writing at City University. The resulting novel, *Frazzlehead* – crime with a reality twist – is now with an agent.

www.finnclarke.com

Solution

Janet Howson

Peter stared out of the steamed-up window of the coffee bar he had retreated to in an attempt to escape from the festive scene outside. He hated Christmas. Well, hate is a strong word. He disliked it intensely. He could willingly list all the reasons for this emotion he had cultivated over the years.

There was a distant memory of a time he had loved Christmas. He could remember being very young, entranced by the lights on the Christmas tree and the red and gold tinsel and numerous golden balls of various sizes draped round it. Paper chains bedecking the walls. Advent calendars and mistletoe hanging from the door jambs and of course, the pile of presents in their bright, gaudy Christmas wrap of reindeers, Father Christmas, elves and snowmen. The excitement in his stomach at the thought of Father Christmas coming down the chimney with a sack full of presents just for him. He remembered leaving out the obligatory mince pie and glass of sherry for Father Christmas and a carrot for Rudolph.

When did it all tarnish, this glossy view? Peter supposed it started once he knew that Father Christmas and Rudolph the reindeer were all fictional. The shocking truth being imparted to him by his peer group at school who had older brothers and sisters. Being mocked for still believing it all.

He continued loving Christmas Day for a long time. The dinner cooked by his mum. Turkey and all the trimmings followed by a steamed pudding with a coin wrapped in foil that always seemed to end up on his plate. The Christmas crackers containing a terrible joke and a paper hat that had to be worn until bedtime. Playing board games and listening to the Queen's speech and of course, being allowed to stay up late.

Peter leafed through his paper and found the crossword page with the cryptic clue he had been unable to complete. He prided himself on completing this crossword every day. He was stuck on nine across, eight letters with the clue: *This starts without relevance and ends with a question surrounding computer speak and victory leading to a birth.*

The only letter he had got was a 't' from the answer of another clue. He had gone back and forward to it all day but had got no further.

Peter's mind drifted back to Christmas and the list of reasons he did not enjoy it. This had been spurred by the Christmas music on a loop in the coffee bar, whilst nursing a large cup of extra hot latte. The droning of *I Wish It Could Be Christmas Every Day*, *I'm Dreaming of a White Christmas*, *Wish I Could Be Home for Christmas* and all the rest, invading the small space, much too loud. This had come after ploughing through the shops with similar music, just as loud, displaying their two-for-one offers, pre-Christmas sales and rack upon rack of ideas for presents for family and friends. Crowds of potential customers and habitual browsers, wrapped in thick coats, hats, scarves and gloves, elbowed their way through the hoards, picking up items, replacing them or stowing them away in metal shopping baskets provided by the particular store they were in. Mayhem!

Another annoyance to Peter was how early it all started. Some shops were displaying Christmas Cards in August. It was absurd. That meant five months out of twelve were infected by Christmas Fever. Peter was not religious but he was also aware that nothing seemed to be mentioned about the birth of Jesus, Wise Men, Joseph or Mary. This was very much a distant consideration when compared to the commercial aspect of it all.

He went back to the crossword. Of course, he was suddenly hit with inspiration. *Ends in a Question.* He remembered a clue like that before it was a '*y*'. He filled it in. So the word ended with '*ty*'.

He looked out of the window. Rain slashed across the glass pane and the sky was grey and threatening. Snow? Peter had never known it to snow on Christmas Day. All the cards depicting snow-covered roofs, snowmen being built in gardens, children with sodden mittens and rosy cheeks throwing snowballs. This never happened on December 25th. It was more likely to be a grey day like today.

"The victory clue is a 'v' for victory." The voice shook Peter out of his contemplation. "I couldn't help reading the clue you had not completed. I am pretty sure that is a 'v'. Can't do any more though."

Peter reread the clue. It was obvious now he knew, he filled it in reluctantly. He liked to complete the crossword without help. "Thank you." He looked up to see the owner of the voice, an elderly man who had been sitting at the adjacent table to his, had gathered up his belongings and was making his way towards the exit. So he now had

----V-TY

It was getting dark. The street lights were on and the pendulous Christmas lights were throwing their illumination onto the sides of the shop buildings. White against black. No coloured ones this year. That was a blessing.

He decided on another coffee, he might be here a while yet. He was determined to solve that clue before he went. There was no queue so he was soon back in his seat with the cardboard mug, displaying white snowflakes on a red background, pen in hand, brow furrowed.

Starts with no relevance. So if it is not relevant it is not suitable? Appropriate? Applicable? What about *"na"* for not applicable? That could be it. He pencilled it in.

NA--V-TY

'Computer speak.' That was definitely not his thing. He hadn't quite caught up yet with the fever for technology, the dependence on mobile phones, iPads, Kindles etc.. They did not have IT lessons when he was at school in the seventies. Could that be it: *'IT'?* It had to be surrounded by the other clues. So one could be after the *'v'* and one before. That would read,

NAITVITY

So that wasn't right. So the first must be back to front, *'ti'.*

NATIVITY

Of course! Birth! Nativity!

It was so obvious once he knew the answer. He should have known it would have a Christmas theme to go along with all the rest of the Christmas paraphernalia he had been suffering all day.

Peter put on his coat, hat and scarf, deposited his newspaper in the bin and made his way out of the coffee bar. As he was leaving, one of the coffee baristas called out, "Have a good Christmas."

"Happy Christmas to you too," Peter responded with some conviction. Well, he had worked out the solution to nine across after all.

About the author
Janet taught Drama and English for 35 years, directing a lot of plays, some of which she wrote herself. She has been spurred to start writing again having found a folder of poetry she had written over the years. She is now enjoying writing short stories with the aim of turning some of them into scripts. She feels as if she is at the start of an adventure and feels very excited about it.

Telling Lies

Paula R C Readman

I rose bleary-eyed and drew back the curtains. The sun, hidden by a dark cloud, burst forth with undimmed splendour. Its rays shone off the wet rooftops, and filled my attic flat with a blinding light. I blinked uncomfortably, and wondered whether I'd dreamt about the unexpected call that shattered my sleep last night.

As I sipped my coffee, I recalled the hastily scribbled note and dropped to my knees. I hunted around my bedside cabinet to locate the torn corner from yesterday's newspaper. During the night, it was the only thing at hand, I could find to write on at short notice. It lay caught between a pile of discarded books and dust balls that had gathered around the leg of my metal bed.

My nerves tingled with excitement as I held the torn corner with the address scribbled on it.

How lucky could I be? I asked myself and then it slowly dawned on me. How did she get my number? And why me?

I dragged on my jeans, and yesterday's shirt. I decided where I was heading it wasn't even worth the hassle of a shave. I slipped a slice of bread into the toaster just as the weather forecast on the radio announced rain for the afternoon.

As I grabbed my battered old trilby and a raincoat, I slipped a Dictaphone and a notebook into its deep pockets, pleased that I didn't have to carry a bag.

After checking my watch, I hurried down the stairs, passing Old Mother Berkeley on the landing below mine.

"Morning Jonathan," she said, pushing her key into her door.

"Good Morning, Mrs Berkeley. Can't stop for a chat, today!"

"My goodness, you youngsters are always in a hurry these days," she called after me.

"The times they're a changing, Mrs Berkeley! We're all fast and furious in the1970s," I shouted as I vaulted over the banister, ran down the last flight and out of the front door.

I dashed to my car, hoping to beat the morning traffic. I planned to leave my car at the railway station and take a train to the nearest station to the rendezvous point. I would then walk the rest of way.

During the short train journey, I took the opportunity to brainstorm some ideas of what I wanted to take away from my encounter. I began to scribble down some questions. Photographs would've added clarity to the article, but I didn't want to risk losing the chance to interview her, so I had left my camera at home. Anyway, it was out of the question, her being on the run.

I can't begin to imagine how she got my number. I couldn't believe she wanted to speak to me, I was fresh out of college, but I understood her need for secrecy.

Of course, I was glad to go along with it. Who wouldn't want a meal ticket to fame and fortune? After all, it's an exclusive headliner, a game changer.

As I stepped off the train, a light shower greeted me. I slipped on my raincoat and pulled the Dictaphone out, checking that the batteries were working and I hadn't forgotten a tape. By the time, I was hurrying along the road the rain bounced off the pavements, roofs, cars and rattled the dustbin lids.

I wasn't sure what to expect when I arrived at my

destination. In all honesty, I could've done with a little more time to do some background digging, as most of what I knew was common knowledge. Her name alone could sum up horror among the masses, but I was sure I could walk away knowing her from a different point of view.

I decided to improvise, realising this was the only opportunity available. Aware that after the event some crucial question would annoyingly spring to mind, which I wished I could've asked.

As I rounded the corner onto the estate, the ground was awash with rain and rubbish. I knew, well, more or less guessed that she would've returned to a similar sort of place where she was born. Creatures of habit look for somewhere familiar to feel at home, and to blend in with their own kind. As Rosie's Cafe came into view, I made a dash for it.

Rosie's cafe seemed to be doing a roaring trade on the dilapidated housing estate. I tried to peer through the misted window, before entering, but the condensation within made it impossible to see anything.

The doorbell rang as I opened the door, making everyone within turn to gape in my direction. As the conversation resumed, I looked around trying to seek out my interviewee.

The cafe's decor was past its best. The walls were covered in laminated wood style panelling that might have been pine-coloured once, but now nicotine-stained orange. The fixed hard orange plastic seating matched perfectly well with the walls and ceiling.

In the damp, stale airless space that stunk of cigarette smoke, greasy fried food and body odour, I glanced around, expecting to see the all too familiar face, once plastered on numerous daily newspapers over the years, but saw no one who fitted the bill.

I crossed to the counter, and ordered a cup of tea and a couple of slices of toast. As I waited, I scanned the room again. In one corner, I noticed a young woman nodding in my direction. She returned my smile. I realised then she had located me first.

On her arrival at the cafe, she seemed to have selected a table nearest to the window that also faced the door. With her back to the wall, she sat the furthest from the draughty door.

I wondered whether her selection had less to do with not wishing to miss me, but more about her self-preservation as the seat gave her the clearest view of the room. Maybe, a past habit learnt out of necessity.

After paying for my food and drink, I carried them over to her table. Her voice surprised me by its softness.

"You came," she said.

"Yes, why wouldn't I? I'm intrigued, and want to hear your point of view."

Now close up, her haggard features, shocked me, though knowing her dark past, I should have expected it.

"I don't know." She lowered her gaze, staring into her mug of cold coffee.

"Would you like a fresh one?" I asked.

She met my stare, with a candid look of her own, as though I was about to trick her into revealing something unknown about herself. (She seemed to ponder the question, her piercing blue eyes narrowed.)

I smiled, breaking eye contact to show I was allowing her time to decide. I was there for no other reason than she wanted me to be, on her terms, not mine. As my frayed nerves began to relax, I leant back in the uncomfortable seat, trying to soak up the atmosphere as I thought about my article.

I wanted to take out my notebook and record every detail, worried that the noise in the cafe would drown out our conversation on the Dictaphone, which was recording in my pocket.

"Yes, I will," she finally said.

Once I had returned to my seat, I slid the mug over to her before taking a sip of my tea. It tasted as bad as it looked somewhere between nicotine orange and the colour of the seat and even tasting like plastic too.

She gave a light laugh. It brightened her face, her eyes softened, making her look younger. "Yes, that's why I only drink the coffee in here."

I grinned at her simple joy, but still saw an aura of sadness within her eyes. The cafe seemed to embrace her. She neither blended in, nor stood out from the crowd in the steamy, stained place.

"I guess you're wondering why I contacted you?" she said with a sharpness in her tone.

I gave a nod, saying nothing as I nibbled on the dry toast.

"I've decided I can't run and hide forever, so I wanted someone willing to listen to me. I'm starting a new life soon. It won't be easy for me even though I've paid society back for what I've done. For others, no matter what I do, it won't be enough, I know."

I pushed the toast away and took another sip of my drink, before answering, "I do understand that, it can't be easy for you."

"Do you?" She gestured palms up.

I suddenly became aware I was staring at her hands.

As though reading my mind, she pulled the sleeves of her jumper down, hiding her hands out of sight.

I cursed my stupidity, fearing she might leave.

She leaned forward, her lips parted slightly. I inhaled and held my breath, willing her to continue, and not to say, "I've made a terrible mistake, I'm sorry I've nothing more to say to you."

Suddenly the doorbell rang loudly, silencing the conversation in the cafe as the wind and rain drove in another customer.

As a flash of fear crossed the young woman's face, she bit her bottom lip. I turned, and saw everyone looking in the direction of the door.

"A bloody awful day," the new arrival said to no one in particular. Without glancing around, the old man wiped the rain from his grimy face and ordered a drink.

The people nearest him nodded in agreement and returned to their conversations. As the noise rose to its normal level again, I turned to my companion.

"You need to understand," she said softly. "I'm frightened of leaving, after being institutionalised for so long."

"In what way frightened?" I asked. "Surely you're looking forward to being free again."

"Free." She laughed. "I shall never be free. Did you know I must create a new past for myself? How are you supposed to remember all the lies you have to tell others? Of course, there are some things you can't easily leave behind when the whole bloody world seems to know more about you than you do yourself.' She took another sip of her drink. "Are you going to take this down?"

Her question startled me out of my thoughts. "Oh yes, if you don't mind?"

"It's why you're here." She looked around as though she had spoken too loud.

149

I pulled out my notebook, checking my Dictaphone was still on.

She lowered her mug. "I wanted someone to hear my point of view, in my own words. Can I trust you?"

"Yes, of course you can," I lied, wondering if I should warn her that my editor might want me to elaborate on parts of my article, making changes. As I had no means of contacting her, I wouldn't be able to ask her permission.

Her eyes narrowed. Somehow, within them a look of innocence radiated back at me beyond the years that marked her face.

I reminded myself of the fact there were lives taken far too soon. Yet within her deep blue pools of darkness, I saw a haunted lost childhood too. Those who should've cared for her failed, marring her life forever. The wisdom that resided in her, many of us couldn't comprehend, nor deal with. Yet here she sat, asking for my trust.

"I'm not sure what you're asking of me," I said, licking the end of my pencil then wishing I hadn't. I took a sip of the disgusting tea.

"I am entrusting you to tell the truth," she said.

"Of course, it's my job. So explain what exactly I'm recording."

"My transition. My past is public knowledge. After today, I'm reborn. It's my nativity. I want to be free to start anew, no more reporters hounding me. The only person telling lies about me will be me," she whispered.

I sat staring at my pencil tip as the words she spoke appeared like magic on the page, all her bottled up hopes and fears for the future.

"Your past gives you your identity, as much as we may wish to escape it. All those familiar, comforting things from your childhood, your home, and even the street you've lived on, I've lost." She drained her mug.

I stopped writing, and looked up.

"I know what you're thinking," she said.

I laid my pencil down. "Do you now? You can't possibly."

"I've seen that same look in others' eyes, their unspoken rebuke. They don't see why I should live after what I've done." She sighed, and pushed her mug away. "I've paid my dues. Don't you think if it were possible for me to undo what I did, I would've done it by now?"

I nodded.

"I've accepted the consequences of my actions. I'm not proud of them, but why should I have to lie? I want so much to be honest to tell the truth should the moment arise, and be able to hang my head in shame. But instead, I have to hide away otherwise another life is at risk?"

"You mean your own?"

"No. I'm aware that others wish me dead. If someone were to kill me then my death would be at the destruction of another family. It wouldn't resolve anything." She lowered her eyes, wiping away a tear. "I've accepted that I must live a lie now."

I looked down at my notebook. Questions were beginning to form in my head. "So you've taken on a new name?"

She glanced around, but no one seemed to be particularly interested in us.

"Yes, I've quite enjoyed researching one. It made me wonder about my parents. You know, whether they chose my name together before I was born, or was it an afterthought. Why did they settle on the one, they gave me? Maybe, if I'd had a different name, I might've developed into someone else." She peered into her empty mug as though forgetting she had finished her drink. "It's a pity that we don't get a clean slate to go with a new name as we did when we're christened."

"Does your new name fit you yet?"

She smiled as though waiting for me to ask what it was. I wasn't going to, nor had I planned to either.

"No, it doesn't. It's just a face in a mirror with a name that doesn't fit. As any woman will tell you, we have to make changes to our appearance to conform to the latest fashion. So it was easier enough for me to make changes to my appearance to lose my identity. It makes you realise just how shallow fashion is when you need to reform your existence to live a lie," she said, glancing around the room, before continuing. "From the colour of my eyes to the mole on my left cheek, which once I was so proud of, seeing it as a mark of beauty, now marks me out as a killer. I'm not just a wronged lover, or a killer in self-defence. No, I'm the lowest of the low, a child killer. Oh, your eyes speak volumes, Mr Reporter. I sense you backing away as though I'm contaminating you and your world."

I paused in my scribbling, fearing my face had revealed too much after hearing her speak her label aloud. Those dreaded words no mother wants to hear. "Hmm, would you like another drink? I know I could do with one."

She nodded.

Once back at the table, I pushed a drink and a chocolate biscuit towards her, trying to think of a question to get the conversation flowing again, but I needn't have worried.

"Of course, you'll question everything I've told you." She took a sip of her drink, before biting into the biscuit.

"Can a leopard change its spots?" Without thinking the question that had been floating around in my head, I spoke aloud.

She leant over the table, her eyes locked on mine. "Why do you think I'm on the run now?"

Her breath caressed my lips. It smelt of coffee mingled

with chocolate. I wanted to lean back, to pull away, but was terrified she'd see it as another rejection. So instead, I focused on the tip of my pencil, and asked, "I was wondering that myself. Why take the risk when you're so close to your release date?"

"I just wanted to walk the streets unknown. To be myself for a while before the reporters knew about my release." She gave a light laugh. "As strange as it may seem, I hate this freedom, and feel torn to shreds inside without an identity."

"So you're going back?"

"As soon as we've finished our coffees and talking."

We both took a sip of our drinks. She was right, the coffee was mildly better. Not an expensive brand, but good quality nonetheless.

A sort of silence… no more than a mutual peace settled between us as we enjoyed our coffees.

An unexpected shaft of sunlight hit our table and we both glanced towards the window. As I turned back I realised she was heavily made-up, the powder so thick it seemed the change the shape of her face. I wondered if, sometime in the future, she would feel relaxed enough to be herself again. I become aware she was intensively studying me too, so I smiled.

She nodded and then glanced over her shoulder, making sure no one was listening. "I've always found it fascinating why others find my story so appealing. What drives their need to know?"

I shook my head.

"Oh, I can understand why psychiatrists, doctors or police all want to know what motivates a child killer," she went on, "but don't you think it's somewhat sickening the way others want to know all the gory details? I've always believed it's some sort of voyeurism which makes the general public want to know every sickening details of what happened to the children. It's as though they gain some pleasure from knowing what's happened, without suffering the consequences of their action."

I felt a chill run down my back, and lifted my pencil from the page. "Maybe they're just curious to know what lead you to..." I hesitated.

"What made me cross the line?" she said, with a cold smile.

"Yes. Most of us don't. We get angry, utter words, a threat, but we don't."

She lowered her eyes, her voice no more than a whisper. "You're all searching for the truth. You want reassurance you don't have it in you to do the same. Did you know, there's only a millisecond between an action and its result? Just think there the pressure on a trigger, the arc of a blade, or a droplet of poison, which marks the distance between turning back and game over." She met my gaze, her eyes narrowed, a thin smile played on her red lips. "There was no demon in me, no voice of god telling me to do it. I was a child, no thoughts behind my actions. The truth is I just did it. I crossed a forbidden line."

We stepped out into the sunshine, and said our goodbyes. As I watched her walk away, I felt torn between doing my job and my conscience as her words echoed in my head.

"Were we all just searching for truth with our fascination in horrific crimes, or were we just voyeurs enjoying the suffering of others?"

I slipped my hand into my pocket, pulled out my notebook, and discovered that the tape in my Dictaphone had unravelled. As I headed for the train, I wondered if the forces of circumstance had made the decision for me.

154

About the author

Paula R.C. Readman was the overall winner of the Writing Magazine/Harrogate Crime Writing Festival Competition, when the crime writer Mark Billingham selected her dark crime story, *Roofscapes*. Since 2013, she had twenty-eight other short stories published in anthologies and online and is now working hard to get her first crime novel published.

Paula has an Amazon Author page, and a blog:
http://paulareadman1.wordpress.com

The Go Girl

I L Green

"I'm not what you would call socially proficient."

"I know the feeling," Iris said. "I hate these group projects."

"It's always the same," Zach said. "One person takes charge. Someone does all the work. And there's the ones who do little to nothing."

"That's us," Iris laughed.

"But we're here at least. We show up. I'm giving them another fifteen minutes."

"Then we go to my car and get high."

The coffee house chosen for the meeting was small and overcrowded.

"What is this shit music they're playing?" Iris complained.

"It's called coffee-shop. It's an actual genre."

She grimaced. Iris was twenty years Zach's junior. They spent the past semester in Abnormal Psych class together. She always dressed the same. T-shirt, Vans, skinny jeans, and a brown slouch beanie. Zach always looked old and haggard, somehow adorable. The worse he looked the more she was enamoured of him.

"Nativity time?"

"That's the go phrase. That phrase activates the plan. Not a text message, or phone call. It has to be face to face. We have to be able to look the other in the eye and say it. We have to be in it together or we don't go at all."

"You're that writer guy." Iris said matter-of-factly.

"I am?"

"The one my English teacher is always talking about. You just sold the rights to your novel to some big studio in Hollywood?"

"It sounds sinful the way you say it."

"Aren't you excited?"

"It was actually optioned by a small production company that contracts for a big studio. I'm not excited, cause I have to fly out there. A condition for the sale is that I sign on as a creative consultant."

"Wow! You need an assistant?"

"I'm not leaving until after the semester. My boss said to not show up alone though: bring someone with me from home. Since my wife died nine months ago she feels it's a bad time for me to travel alone, but the production has already started. So what I need is an executive proxy," Zach declared.

"Like an assistant."

"No. There's plenty of those out there on the west coast. I can get my own coffee. I need someone to work on the project and be able to make executive decisions and take creative action on behalf of my work. Someone from home who is smart and badass like yourself, who I can trust."

"So we'll have to work pretty closely together?"

"No again. We'll work separately for Natalie who heads the production company. We really won't need to talk or see each other."

"I don't understand."

"I have anxiety issues. I may not always be able to attend meetings, especially with the suits from the studio. Natalie won't hire me without a backup from my home. An executive proxy. Someone who can fill in at any time to do my job."

"Wow."

"Yeah, and now that you bring it up I think you'll do perfectly. I get to choose, but Natalie will have the final word."

"But I don't need to work with you?"

"We can talk, we can be friends. But she really wants someone able to act on their own who understands the project."

"No packing or saying goodbye. We leave no matter what's happening, together to the storage unit and get the bugout bag, pay cash for a used nondescript car and drive away."

Zach spent the remainder of the semester never bringing up the subject again to Iris. He wasn't against hiring her as an executive proxy, but she initiated the conversation and he wanted her to return to the subject on her own, in a way to prove she was serious and not just some flibbertigibbet kid only looking out for the next fun adventure. This was serious to him and it had to be serious for her.

By the end of the semester they both found themselves in front of the psychology class ready to give a presentation that neither one had helped with or practiced. Iris was flipping through index cards in her hands pretending to put them in some sequential order that would benefit her part in the presentation. The cards actually held the secret recipes to her mother's baking success that Iris had lifted from the kitchen so that she would look professional in front of the class.

"You still going west superstar?" Iris asked playfully while everyone was still mulling around the room setting up PowerPoint slides and making sure they knew their points.

"Are you ready for this?" Zach asked.

"Ready as I need to be. I aced the final for this class and don't really need a good grade on the presentation."

"You played the 'what do I need to pass' game?" Zach chided.

"All it takes is a calculator."

"Aren't you afraid of being embarrassed, you know, lack of preparation?"

"I never get embarrassed."

They met after, for old time's sake, in Zach's truck to smoke some weed and celebrate passing the semester of community college.

"So yeah, I'm leaving in a week for the promised land," Zach said.

"The offer still on the table, remember, executive assistant?"

"Yeah it is."

"So you were just leaving without talking to me?"

"I figured you'd bring it up soon. I wanted to make sure you really wanted to go."

"I've told my mother I'm going. I actually have a bag packed."

"Wow! Shit, okay; then I have to show you something." Zach turned the ignition on the truck and kicked it into gear. They ended up on a dark isolated country road far from the city, yet Iris was not nervous. She trusted Zach, and she still had her phone with her that had a strong signal.

"So what's the deal with this place?" Iris asked.

She was investigating the inside of a large desolate farmhouse that Zach had taken them to. It looked clean and smelled of fresh paint. She turned off the flashlight on her phone when Zach lit an oil lamp.

"I bought this," Zach answered. "With the payoff for my novel."

"Kinda bleak…"

The lights weren't on and the rooms of the house they occupied were void of furniture. Zach had lit a kerosene lamp on the kitchen counter. The little flame danced with the air back and forth under its glass cover, casting animated dark shadows of them against the walls in the room.

"Well I haven't moved in yet. But it's everything I ever

wanted. Two-story farmhouse surrounded by cornfields, ten miles away from the nearest neighbour. Wrap around porch. Woods with a stream on the property. Diesel powered generator, wind and solar energy. No phone or Wi-Fi."

"You got some poor girl held hostage in the basement?"

"It's a safe house Iris."

"Now I am creeped out."

"This was my childhood home, I was born here in this very room. So was my father and my grandmother. Dad lost the place in the 80s cause of bad health and, well, it was the 80s.

"I get that," Iris explained. "But what do you need to be safe from?"

"We Iris, we need to be safe. Before we catch the plane west I wanted to talk to you. Give you a chance to make a real informed decision. So I brought you here to the place where I was born to show you where we can be safe, if we need to.

"It's like this, all the popular mean kids we knew from high school graduated and moved to LA, and that's where we're headed. That's who we'll be working with. You can act as tough as you want but it's not our kinda place."

"We'll have a contract right?"

"It won't be enough. We need a plan. We need to make a promise to each other."

Iris and Zach joined pinky fingers in agreement.

"Sign on the line and I own you for two years." Their new boss Natalie handed a pen to Iris, who looked at Zach with apprehension on her face. She was somewhat intimidated by the woman she had just met, who owned the production company and held the purse strings for her new job. Iris' small pouty mouth drawn up, grey eyes intense, blonde hair protruding from under her hat. Natalie also slid the half million dollar check across the desk in her direction.

Iris glared intently at the check on the table. It was a hard decision for one so young and far from home; life changing. Taking that kind of money was an act from which most people never returned. Zach had prepped her in advance though. They had agreed to leave behind the money and recognition at a moments' notice and at the bequest of the other. He had forced her to realize before this moment that this business was a construct. Numbers in an account that can be deleted as easily as they were entered. That this could be their home, these people could be friends, or they could return to safety at any time. A contingency Zach feared most people never made in advance to starting on the hero's journey, that home could be decided as the final goal.

"I'm in," Iris declared. She extended her pinky finger in his direction. Zach attached his same finger to hers. She shook it, let go, signed the contract, swooped up the check, and made a hasty exit alone.

"That was interesting," Natalie observed.

"She's in."

"You guys have some deal?"

"To make the money…"

Natalie gave him a discerning look. Long strands of soft dark hair framed a face composed of movie star features. A dazzling smile highlighted by soft brown eyes and high cheekbones leading to a strong jawline that ended with a square chiselled chin. Something didn't sit right with this. But she had no choice. The project was on, and Iris seemed to be 'in'.

They won't come after us. There's no interest searching around fly over states for a couple hack writers. We can lay low in the nativity house for a bit before we part ways…

The duo not only were paid handsomely for their services to Natalie's production company but she also flipped the bill for a two bedroom apartment in the valley they could stay in while working on the film project. The expectation was soon evident that Natalie felt free to use their apartment as she felt fit as a quick location for planning strategies that often involved take-out food and more than occasionally intoxicated sleep overs. The main abusers of these actions being Natalie herself and her comrade Kristen, an actor friend who became involved in the project.

This was how Zach found himself at the moment, alone with the two women and sans Iris who was on a personal errand that left a sick sinking feeling in his gut. In this city it was easy to find any so-called film artist who was nothing more than a predatory con man using his illicit talents on young girls like Iris for various reasons, none of which ever led to an actual paying gig.

Just as Zach was eyeing the text app on his phone Iris burst into the apartment, interrupting the impromptu meeting Natalie had called. She was sobbing, black mascara running down her face. Red lipstick was smeared on her mouth, cheeks, and chin. Small drops of blood splattered her white strapless evening gown. She stopped in front of Zach and composed herself momentarily. "I'm going to get cleaned up."

"Could you grab my sunglasses on your way out?"

Kristen looked astonished at Zach. "Sunglasses?"

"I'll need them."

"Are you heartless? Go see what's wrong with her. Where the hell was she?"

"I'm not sure, some photoshoot or video thing. Looks like it went afoul," Zach studied his phone as a blasé kind of distraction.

"She needs you," Kristen insisted. She shared Iris' blond hair colour and grey eyes that nearly turned green in the sunlight. She was short though, like Natalie, but didn't share her movie star facial features. Her bread and butter rose from a strong ability as a thespian and a body designed by Venus herself to attract and entrap all who were fortunate enough to have her gaze fall on them.

"She'll come get me when she needs me."

"You guys are so weird. I need to go find out what happened," Kristen declared.

"Leave her be."

"She's clearly a mess!"

"She's the strong silent type. She knows what to do."

"Sunglasses," Kristen reiterated. Her eyes narrowed disapprovingly on Zach who tried not to notice. He looked at Kristen finally and hoped his angst wasn't showing. She was the strong silent type too. Her hair had been shaved for the last movie project she had worked on. The look leant her a hardness Zach wasn't used to. Intense eyes stared him down under blonde eyebrows.

"This isn't right," Kristen continued. "Youngsters need someone to check on them. You share this apartment. I thought you two were pretty tight."

"We don't see much of each other."

Everyone was silent for a few very long moments. They could hear the shower running through the walls.

"I somehow doubt that," Natalie said finally breaking the silence. "In the middle of the night when you're scared and it's dark, you reach out for the person close to you. I know how this works. Hang out at the barbershop long enough and you're bound to get a haircut."

Zach lowered his eyes trying to not give anything away. He knew Iris was finished and what was coming. He did like these people. He wanted the meeting to continue, wanted them to keep the creative juices flowing. Working out the details of the project. Another sleepover was on tap and he was about to miss out on it.

"Roommates," he offered. "You know how it goes. She has her thing and I got mine."

"You hate it here don't you?" Natalie asked, her dark eyes searching for what Zach was hiding. "You Midwesterners are all the same. Just can't take the heat."

"I made it a year. I can go another."

"What about Iris?"

"Iris is a country girl. Her heart will always belong to the deciduous forest. She might be young and star struck out here, but she knows where she's from. The camera flash never overpowers the chime of the birth chord."

"Where's your heart Zach?" Kristen asked. "It's obvious we'll never get to keep you here."

"The far side of the long golden prairie."

"What's there that we don't have here?" Natalie asked.

Zach was a bit surprised at what seemed like negotiating on the parts of his work partners. It had now been almost two years since the death of his beloved wife, and these girls had gone to extraordinary lengths to make him feel at home. There seemed to be an agreement of ownership of his person between them. At what point had they decided he was staying?

"If you've never tasted that sweet country air then we don't share a point of reference."

Iris entered the room. Black t-shirt, Vans, and skinny jeans. Her familiar brown slouch beanie on her head. Sunglasses covered what her eyes gave away. "Nativity time," she announced to Zach.

Kristen's jaw dropped. Her eyes met with Natalie's as the two intuitively figured out what was happening. This was now the young girl who first appeared in Natalie's office too scared to touch a bonus check.

164

"She's your go girl," Kristen announced in a low airy breath, almost a whisper.

"I should have seen this coming," Natalie declared. "This is a mistake Zach. You walk out that door and your contract will be nullified. The project will proceed without you and your name will be nowhere to be found on this film."

"No credit," Kristen admonished. "No recognition!"

Zach stood and put on his sunglasses, he had a promise to keep and promises carried a stronger form of currency that had nothing to do with bank accounts and sweet Hollywood perks. They opened the door to the bright California afternoon and left the meeting, never to be seen again.

About the author

Iris' history of publications includes Slice Magazine, Downstate Story, Bluffs Literary Magazine, and CaféLit. She is an English/Literature major at Bradley University in Peoria, Illinois and hopes to use her learned skills to enhance her writing ability. Iris lives in an empty nest in the same town as her university with wife Bonz, five dogs, and three exotic, though unwieldy, birds. Her novel *Redemption Story*, published by Czykmate Productions, is currently available at Amazon: https://smarturl.it/opn6ra.

The Legionary

Nicolas Siregar

8 BCE
Bethlehem, Provincia Iudea

"Of all the blasted places in our great Republic, why must we be stationed here?" muttered Marcus Decius, a legionary of the Legio X Frateris, given the post of night's watchmen just outside the camp. It was cold, dark, and most importantly, mind numbingly boring…

Decius was born a to an impoverished plebeian community, he joined the legion as an alternative to starving in the streets, and he'd been in this job for the past 10 years… and it was much less exciting than he thought it would be.

When Decius first joined, he thought he'd be fighting alongside his comrades for the glory of Rome, smiting what surely would be new challengers to the Imperator, or perhaps against those Parthians to the East, or perhaps some troublesome Germanic tribes!

But the civil wars were done and over, the Republic was at peace, and the Shahansha of the Parthians were not inclined to do battle with Rome as many would have thought, and the tribes? Not a word since the time of the traitor Arminius. And so, for the past ten years he was mostly relegated to guard duty.

The only time there was something even close to battle was during his time in Jerusalem, barely a few months ago. There was, what he can only describe, as a spontaneous riot amongst the populace… He'd rather not think too much about it…

And thus, Decius was stationed here, in sleepy

Bethlehem… a small, backwater town in the middle of literal nowhere, where, at most, there was only the sound of camels, carts, and the occasional "TWANG!" of blacksmiths hammering in their smiths.

So much for 'defending Rome's glory'. At times, when he stood guard, he felt less like a defender of the Roman Republic and more like a paid guard dog.

Hours passed… He could feel his eyelids get heavier. The only thing keeping him awake was fear of the Centurion (who would give him a thorough beating for negligence… at best). Truly this was by far the worst assignment that any legionary could ever have and ever will have.

But… Decius had an inkling feeling that something DEFINITELY felt off…

Perhaps it was instinct, like how a deer tenses up when it senses danger, or perhaps it was the odd, faint, sound that – in the midst of the rather erratic symphony of Bethlehem nights – was as piercing through his ears like a pilum punching itself through a wooden shield. He had to investigate it, for all his complaints of his post, he absolutely cannot let a potential threat do harm to the men.

He steadily marched to the direction of the sound, praying to the gods to give him strength, just in case this WAS more than just a bandit looking to steal some rations.

Then he heard the braying… Oh by the gods, what caravan travels to Bethlehem this late at night? They were lucky he was the only one who spotted them. If it were his centurion, he'd probably cause the NEXT major conflict of the century.

"HALT! In the name of Augustus Caesar and 10th Legion! State your intentions lest you need to find an additional set of hands to pickpocket!" bellowed out Decius.

He spotted three figures in the darkness. They appeared to be trying to calm down a donkey.

Decius waved his torch as he approached the interlopers, and as he approached closer the three men seemed to stop whatever they were doing and faced toward him. With the light from the torch in his hand, he could finally see what exactly these men were.

None of the men seemed to be from any province of the Republic, they look more like they come from their eastern neighbours.

Garamantines perhaps? Sabaeans? If they're Parthians then he must take serious precautions before doing anything too rash.

Two of the men looked perplexed, probably trying to assess the situation at hand, but the largest of the men, and who also looked to be the oldest, approached him.

"Fear not, son of Rome, we have no intentions to do you or your legion harm" the man said, with an aura of confidence and even a little mirth.

"You sound as if you are heading to a festival, but there are no festivals in Bethlehem... It's too remote for any travellers of note," Decius told the men.

The man simply laughed.

"Ah, we ARE going to have celebrations, but not one of drink and wine!"

Decius furrowed his brow and scowled.

"Who ARE you... and what is there to celebrate? Almost nothing happens here!"

The wise man simply nodded, with an understanding smile meant to reassure him.

"Ah! Nothing? Oh, on the contrary my good sir, we are here to celebrate the birth of royalty!"

Okay, now Decius was getting pissed off.

"Tell me your name right now lest I remove your head from your shoulders with my bare hands! I swear on the gods..."

The man in front of him didn't even flinch.

"Apologies sir, I have yet to properly introduce myself. My name is Caspar, I am a Magi from Persia, and I have been travelling for months alongside my two compatriots"

There... Finally, some answers, and of course the man would be Persian. Now he was glad he resisted the urge to arrest the men on the spot. But now, that leads to some other questions he's been wondering...

"Magi? So... you're a bunch of wise men from a foreign kingdom, but you do not come to the great cities of the Republic? Why? Would it not be more prudent to go to Jerusalem? It is the centre of power in this province...

Caspar shook his head.

"No, my good man, we are not here for these kings. The petty kings who plunder the lands of smallfolk and take from the needy. No, we are here to celebrate the birth of a king beyond kings"

THAT was dangerous.

"That could have your head on a spike... Do you realize how reckless and stupid that sounds? You would not only make an enemy of Herod's dynasty, but of Rome itself. Do you know who makes kings in these lands? Rome! We ousted our kings to form our Republic, and we certainly would not tolerate a new crown that just popped up from the sands!"

Caspar said nothing, and simply looked at him straight in the eye.

"How about this? If a new dynasty wants to take its place upon the throne of any of our provinces it is through

169

the Augustus! Without us, your kings would be crushed beneath our feet!"

Still nothing.

"Still not convinced of your utter foolishness? Fine! What of your own tribe? The Parthians? The Arsacids will not tolerate a pretender."

Caspar simply shook his head.

"What you talk about is true, but they are simply matters of state, and those are not the matters we are interested at all."

Decius gripped his torch tighter. He was fighting very hard simply not to smack him right here and then.

"Mortal kings come and go, and nations rise and fall. Tell me good sir, do you honestly believe that your Augustus is not a king?"

"Of course not! He is but the Imperator, the first commander of Rome's legions" countered Decius.

"Then why does he send his Legatus to each of his provinces? Are they not the true governors? Why does he have sole power to choose who leads and who doesn't. Your Senate certainly does not lead anymore. Tell me, what power do they have? And I mean real power, not simply pleasantries and shows to convince the masses that everything is fine?"

Decius was quiet this time. It stung, but the Magi had pointed out something that was always lingering on the back of his mind…

"He has sole command of his armies, armies that, mind you, can be sent anywhere at his word. Not his Senate. The governors and all the petty kings are beholden to him! Tell me, are those not the actions of a king?"

Decius gritted his teeth… The Magi must have been trained for this.

"Your republic, the very idea of how your country

works, has traded from one set of rulers to another, single one. It had its time, and now a new form of king has taken its place. Back home it is the Shahansa, here it is the Augustus. In lands where Alexander once marched, it is the Raja. And all of them, in time, will shift into the sands of history. What we have come here goes beyond the authority of kings."

Decius could only sigh.

"What do you mean beyond?"

Caspar replied "The king we are looking for will have no throne in this life, but a throne afterwards. A king that will be remembered by nations all over the world, but is not part of any culture or country. A king that speaks to the destitute and downtrodden, with compassion to their plight."

Decius, remained silent for a while. He could only remember what it was like growing in a slum in Roma, destitute and alone, begging for scraps. He was only able to escape that life by joining the Legions.

And yet, he couldn't possibly put faith in his fellow plebs. After all, he still remembers what happened in Jerusalem.

"What you say about the poor are true. I was a victim of such misfortune, why do you think I donned the gladius? But they are not guiltless either… When I was in Jerusalem, a bunch of plebs loyal to Herod took it upon themselves, after what started as, if my memory serves me… a rumour started in a tanner's shop."

Caspar waited for Decius to continue. After taking a deep breath, Decius recounted one of the worst nights of his life.

"Not all the Judeans were loyal to Herod. Many have never forgiven us for subjugating them… and by extension Herod himself for being a puppet. But even then, Herod

171

certainly has his followers… One day, a group probably too drunk for their own good overheard the tanner complaining about the current state of Judea. The drunkards thought he was trying to oust Herod.

"Imagine that? A tanner? Going up against the king of Judea? You know what they did to the man? They tried to beat him death! A brawl became a small riot, and one of my comrades had to step in to nip this rebellion in the bud. He would never raise his sword for Rome ever again thanks to these small-minded miscreants!"

Decius finally let out his inner anger. It was good to let out his frustrations for once, the gods know he needed that…

"So, let me ask you? What difference would THIS 'king' make? When the small folk are so liable to fall into the same idiocy as the upper crust in all their opulence?"

Caspar was deep in thought… Aha, so he does acknowledge the foolishness of men. The Magi replied thusly.

"I apologize for your tragedy sir. At times, men are prone to idiocy and violence, for reasons that even evade me. Trust me, your Republic is not immune to this, as I, a child of Persia, know all too well about the resentment of the people. Our people have long memories. There are the Seleucid loyalists, and those who feel we simply traded the Macedonian tyrant for one closer to kin."

"But believe me… In the end, it all comes down to one thing. The feeling that the people's needs being unfulfilled and their voices unheard. They look for likeminded voices who share their grievances, and fall prey to those that stoke the worst in them."

"Common men need a guide, to give them hope to trudge through the harshness of life. We believe that the one born in Bethlehem will be that catalyst of hope."

Not wanting to argue any longer, Decius simply sighed. He instead tried a different approach. Though not overtly religious, Decius had the same beliefs and superstitions as the rest of his fellow Romans, and he wanted to understand the spiritual reasons for coming here.

"If I may, Caspar. You are a man of faith, correct? Now, all men of faith in Rome, be it the priesthoods back home or the pharisees here in Judea, all of them look to signs from the gods to give them guidance. Now... good sir... what message did the gods send YOU to march all the way here to Bethlehem?"

Caspar simply smiled.

"Then you might want to look above, my friend. Right behind me."

Decius looked up toward the night sky. Something WAS odd actually. A star, brighter than all the others, shimmered like a firefly on an open grass field. Must be a sign from Fortuna... But why here? Why not a palace, or a port? Or anywhere more substantial really...

"The star shines strongly yes, but what other good portance is there besides its brightness in the night sky?" Decius inquired.

"Look closely at the star. Is it not a strange sight? All the stars in the night sky give it a wide berth, as if though they bow to the Star's presence. Even the moon is not lit during this night... Is that not a curious sign?"

Decius simply nods...

"If I may, you Romans try to understand portance from livers and entrails? Do you not? So how is it any different to use the stars as guides?"

Decius... really didn't know how to reply to that. Though he was not completely religious, even he still acknowledged when it seemed the gods gave a sign.

He sighed... finally relenting.

"Alright foreigner. You have my permission to pass, but you are still under strict supervision. You and your group of friends WILL be escorted to your designation. Pray that you behave, lest you understand the consequences."

Caspar was ecstatic. He hugged his companions as if their lives depended on it.

"Thank you! Thank you so much sir! May God bless you for your understanding!"

Decius' response was to simply nod, and lead them toward the stable. He still found it odd to say the least, and perhaps the three men were just insane... But he made a promise, and by his honour as a Roman and the tenth Legion he will fulfil that that promise.

They arrived just a few meters outside of the stable, and here he and the three Magi would part ways. As Decius bid them farewell and began marching back to his comrades in arms. He couldn't help but look back at the scene.

He could see a child in a manger, alongside the parents. There was an eerie serenity emanating from the family. He could feel some kind of warmth, one that he cannot explain, that the stable radiated from.

Decius' eyebrows lit up when he saw the child being given gifts of gold, frankincense and myrrh. *They really are treating him as a king*, Decius thought to himself.

Whoever this child will be, Decius can only hope that the boy will do good things for the Republic. Who knows? Perhaps the child will change the very face of the Republic, much like Caesar had. He doubts he'd be an Alexander or Augustus, after all, he was but a boy born from what looks to be your average Judean peasant.

As Decius looked up to the star once more, he could only hope that what the Magi said would be true.

Perhaps Bethlehem wasn't such a bad place after all. This night certainly was an eventful one!

About the author

Nicolas Siregar is a Character, Creature designer and Storyboard Artist working in a small animation startup in Jakarta Indonesia. He has a distinct interest in historical writing, and is always interested in writing stories from the perspective of the people who lived there, as well as exploring fantasy and science fiction concepts that take elements from history.

Website:
https://nicolassiregara3d.wixsite.com/nicolassiregarart

The Seventh Angel

Joy Mawby

There are one little, two little, three little angels,
Four little, five little, six little angels,
Seven little...

Where on earth is the seventh Angel? Where is Billy
Grimshaw?

I made sure he was safely between Angel Six, sensible
Jenny Bradley, and Angel Eight, sturdy Martin Dobbs,
when I lined the children up at the classroom door. How
could Billy have escaped?

*There are **ten** little angels in the band,* the angels sing
– but there aren't, are there? There are only nine because
Billy Grimshaw is missing.

I try to catch Maggie's eye but she is too busy pushing
a shepherd on to the stage. You know the one – his tea towel
always slips over his eyes and, if you give him a crook, he
trips up the Angel Gabriel or, worse still, the donkey.
Thinking of donkeys, that's where Maggie said I should put
Billy.

"Back half of a donkey, that's the best place for him,"
she'd said last week. "He can't go far astray there, can
he?"

"But he's got such gorgeous blond curls and blue eyes,"
I'd pleaded. She had cast me a pitying look as she walked
away and, now I realise she was right.

I peer into the hot, over-crowded hall to see if Billy has
ended up with his mother. Parents are packed,
uncomfortably, on infant chairs and are standing along the
back as well. There's no sign of Billy. I spot Mrs
Grimshaw, though, sitting in the front row, arms folded,

looking – well – grim. She's wondering where the bloomin' hell her Billy is. She's wasted a perfectly good pillowcase and a bit of tinsel, off the Christmas tree, for his angel outfit and now he's the only child in the class not on the stage.

There's nothing for it. I'll have to go and search. I send up a silent prayer that nothing will go wrong on my side of the stage and make for our classroom. I go through Year 2 class. It's empty except for their robot which gives me a fright because someone has left it switched on. *"I am a robot, I am a robot, I am…"* but there's no Billy.

I can hear shepherds watching their flocks in the hall as I hurry into Year 1. I am so agitated that the hamster, on its wheel, makes me jump. But there's no Billy.

Now I gather, from the music, that the stand-in Mary is safely delivered of the baby doll. Stand-in because the real Mary has impetigo.

There's just my classroom to check. It's empty, strewn with clothes. The only sound is a bluebottle which is hovering above the lunch boxes. Now I hear the *We Three Kings* music as the said kings present the cardboard boxes which I painstakingly covered in shiny paper and glitter during the evenings of last week. I know I have about four minutes to find Billy and get him on the stage before the grand finale. I turn to go. Where can I look now?

Then I hear a tiny noise, a sort of sigh. I rush to the corner of the classroom, peer over the top of the playhouse and, yes, there's Billy Grimshaw fast asleep. His thumb is in his mouth. He is an angelic sight if ever I saw one. I bend double to get through the door.

"Billy," I whisper. Then louder, "Billy, wake up, Billy, Billy, wake up!" His eyelids flutter, his eyes open. "Oh Billy," I'm kneeling now. He opens his eyes and stares at me for a moment. "Billy, come on. It's your turn on the stage."

"Don't wannoo."

He closes his eyes. I shake him gently.

"Come on Billy. Mummy's in the hall. She wants to see you."

"Don't wannoo go on the stage. I want my mum"

"Yes, you'll see your mum when you're on the stage," I hiss. "Just come to the hall with me first and sing the angel song and then you can go home with mummy."

"Don't wannoo sing."

"Come on Billy." I lift him up. "Just one little song."

"No"

I sidle past the edge of the playhouse, Billy in my arms Any minute, the angel finale music will strike up and it will be too late I must get Billy on the stage. I'm desperate. I carry him towards the hall as I make my offer.

"Billy, if you go on the stage and sing, I'll give you a lollipop."

There's a pause, then, "Only one lollipop?"

"I'll give you two lollipops."

"Two *red* lollipops?"

"Yes, two red ones."

"All right then. I'll sing."

"Good boy!" We're there, at the side of the stage. I push him into the angel line. Jenny Bradley sees him and pulls him next to her.

"Where've you been?" whispers Martin Dobbs. Billy doesn't answer.

Mrs Grayson starts the final songs. The ten angels are standing behind a bench at the back. Mary and Joseph are in front with the baby. Shepherds, with lambs stand on the right. Kings and pages stand left and the donkey peers over Mary's shoulder. Everyone in the hall joins in the carol, *Away in a Manger*. Then, to finish our Nativity Play the angels sing their song. One by one, as each number is sung, each angel springs up on to the bench and lifts his or her arms up high to form a glorious angel backdrop.

Wasn't there a band on Christmas morning,
Wasn't there a band on Christmas morning,
Wasn't there a band on Christmas morning,
Oh what an angel band!
There are one little, two little, three little angels,
Four little, five little, six little angels,
Seven little, eight little nine little angels,
Ten little angels in the band.

Perfect.

There is a moment's silence. Grannies and granddads wipe tears from their eyes. Even Mrs Grimshaw has softened. Then, before the applause has time to get underway, one loud, clear voice rises from the angelic host, "Miss, can I have my two red lollipops *now*?"

About the author
Joy runs a writing group on the Island of Anglesey, North Wales. She has written three books comprising other people's memoirs, and is completing a personal memoir for her grandchildren. She has written two plays which were performed locally and also writes poetry and short stories. She has headed a team which produced two anthologies of work by local authors and organised a successful writing festival.

The Trip To Nativity

Jim Bates

We'd always been close, my son and I, but in the last few months, ever since he'd started fifth grade, it seemed like we'd been drifting apart. My wife said to be patient, that we'd just hit a bit of a rocky patch, and she was probably right, but the reality was that we just weren't communicating as well as we used to. I didn't like it, but tried, like she said, to be patient.

It turns out she was right. In December, when I picked Ned up at school, he unexpectedly turned to me and asked, "Dad, where'd you grow up again?"

Happy for him to have suddenly initiated a conversation, I quickly responded, "In a small town in central Minnesota. A couple hours west of here." I hardly ever talked about my past around home, but the fact that my son might be interested to know more about it gave me an idea. "How'd you like to drive out there and see it sometime?"

I'd taken a chance. He could always say no and we'd be right back to the way things had been – deafening silence. But, the fact was, I hadn't been back to my hometown for a number of years, ever since Mom had died. A road trip might be in order and give Ned and me a chance to rekindle our relationship.

He surprised me when he turned and grinned. "Sure. That'd be cool."

Well, there you go, you never know until you ask. So on a Saturday, two days before Christmas Eve, we headed for Nativity.

My Grandparents had been farmers for most of their lives. They'd milked nearly one hundred head of dairy cows on forty acres of rolling farmland north of the Minnesota

180

River outside the small town of Nativity, Minnesota. You might have heard of it. It's the town that pulls out all the stops and does lighted nativity displays every Christmas. Almost every home takes part, and it's a pretty big deal. When my grandparents became too old to farm, they moved into town and opened up an antique store, McMahon's, which is still in operation today. They ran it until they passed away. Then my parents took over until they died. Now my second cousin and his wife are the owners.

Growing up, I'd liked living in Nativity in some respects, but I'd also been born with a restlessness that couldn't be contained by a small town out in the middle of rural Prairie County, a county known for producing massive amounts of feed corn and soybeans. I moved away after high school and never looked back. I'd always loved books so I went to college at the University of Minnesota, graduated with a Bachelor of Arts degree and got a job teaching. I've taught eleventh grade American Literature at Southwest High School in Minneapolis for the past eighteen years. This trip would be the first time my ten-year-old son had ever seen where I grew up.

After a two hour drive, I spent about ten minutes touring the back roads south of Nativity showing Ned the country and where my grandparents' farm had been. I guess from his perspective, once you'd seen one wood frame farmhouse and one snow covered field with corn stubble in it, you'd seen them all. Even though he was trying to be polite, I could sense his growing disinterest.

"Well, let's head into town," I finally said. "I'll show you around. How'd you like that?"

He brightened up considerably. "That'd be great."

We rolled into town in the early afternoon. Nativity has a population of around two thousand and is as thriving a community as one could expect given a town that size;

maybe even more so, now that I think about it. The inhabitants are blue collar and salt of the earth. Trust me, I'm not romanticizing the place, they are a hard working lot: grain mill laborers and retired farmers, mostly, with a smattering of independent, self-employed welders, plumbers and electricians. I think the notoriety of the holiday nativity displays helps. People come from all over the upper Midwest during the Christmas season to view them.

We drove down Main Street, past Hendrickson's Hardware, Annie's Bakery and Don's Appliances. The Prairie Sky movie theatre was still in operation, as was Ed's Barber Shop, and Jorgenson's Dry Goods, the store that I remembered for selling everything from work boots and bolts of fabric, to prescription medications and penny candy. Even the town library that first fostered my love of books was still thriving. Basically, nothing had changed.

Snow from a recent storm was piled up along the curbs and evergreen garlands decorated the lamp posts. Every shop and store had brightly coloured lights wrapped around the windows and somewhere someone had set up an outdoor speaker that was playing Christmas carols.

Ned is small for his age, a thin, freckled redhead who needs to wear glasses, and his eyes were wide with wonder as he squirmed back and forth in his seat taking in the sights. It was nice to see his enthusiasm. In the middle of town I pointed out McMahon's, the old family antique store. I was thinking about stopping in when Ned suddenly pointed and said, "Dad, look at that."

I looked. Down a side street and a block over was the city park, and next to the band shell was a horse drawn carriage. It looked like someone was giving rides. Ned surprised me by saying, "That looks pretty cool, Dad. Can we go on it? Please?"

You could have knocked me over with a feather. I'd

never once considered that my son, whose two loves in life were playing baseball and anything on the X-Box, would be interested in something as, shall I say, unexciting, as a carriage ride. But I was wrong. He was, and that got me in the mood, too.

"Sure," I said, smiling at him. "Let's do it."

We parked and walked over to meet the driver. He was a friendly old man with a long white beard and red stocking cap. He warmly shook our hands and introduced himself as Bob. His horse was a big black gelding called Frisky. "His name's a bit of a misnomer," Bob remarked with an endearing chuckle. "But what he lacks in speed, he makes up for by being reliable and steady." He patted Frisky on the flank and added, "Aren't you boy?" The horse whinnied in return.

Well, that's all we needed. We bundled up in thick, wool blankets that smelled faintly of horse (an aroma that was surprisingly pleasing), and Bob and Frisky set out walking at a leisurely pace, clip-clopping down Main Street, bells jingle-jangling from Frisky's leather harnesses. People waved at us from the sidewalks, and we waved back. Next to me, Ned grinned. It was clear he was having a great time.

When we were done touring downtown, Bob turned Frisky toward the quiet streets and quaint neighbourhoods nearby. It didn't take long to get to my old house, a well-maintained two-story structure, built in the style of (what else?) a farmhouse. As we drove by, I asked Bob to stop. When I told him my parents and I had once lived there he was more than gracious. "Jack and Arlene were your folks?" He grinned as I nodded yes. "I knew them," he said. "They were good people."

Next to me Ned leaned over and whispered, "They sound nice. I wish I could have met them."

I fought back a sudden wave of nostalgia and said, "I wish you could have, too, Ned. They would have loved

183

you." I took a moment to collect myself and added, "Like Bob said, they were good people."

Ned smiled at me, and, in that moment, something came over me. I had a sudden urge to hug him, so I did. He didn't resist. In fact, he hugged me back.

Bob giddy-upped to get Frisky going again, and we made our way back to the park. By now the sun had sunk low in the sky and evening twilight was enveloping us. There was a lavender glow in the western horizon, and the air was cold and crisp and still, accented by a faint aroma of wood smoke. One by one, as if by magic, the lighted nativity displays began to come on, reflecting off the snow and casting pools of light into the townsfolk's front yards. Soon, all of Nativity, it seemed, was glowing with an ethereal, magical light.

Ned was enthralled. "Dad, this is so cool."

"It is," I said, almost speechless, looking around in awe, suddenly overcome with feelings of warmth and good cheer. "I'm glad we're here," I whispered to myself.

"Me, too," Ned said.

I hadn't realized he'd heard me. We looked at each other grinning, experiencing a shared bond we hadn't felt in months. It was deep and close, like parent and child close, or father and son close. Maybe even closer.

We said good-bye to Bob and Frisky and watched as they loaded up some more passengers. I thought for a moment, then asked, "Ned, are you cold?" The temperature was in the low twenties, but with the sun going down it felt colder.

"Naw," he grinned. "I'm good." We were dressed for the winter weather in warm boots, heavy jackets, mittens, scarves and knit wool hats. He was watching a group of kids playing hockey on a skating rink in the middle of the park. "I'm not cold at all."

"How about if we got for a walk?"

"Sure. That'd be fun."

"Let's go, then," I said, and off we went, walking through some of the same neighbourhood streets Bob and Frisky had taken us on. It felt good to be out in the invigorating air and stretching our legs. We even went by my folk's old house again. This time there was a man outside making some adjustments with his nativity display while a little girl played in the snow near him. They both waved as we walked by, and we waved back.

"Happy holidays!" Ned called out.

"Happy holidays!" came their friendly response.

It was completely dark when we made our way back to Main Street, and by now we'd worked up a healthy appetite. "You hungry? How about if we get ourselves something to eat?" I asked Ned.

"Sure, that'd be great. I'm starving."

We went into the Blue Dot Diner. It was crowded and hot, with moisture condensing and dripping down the inside of the windows. I could just barely make out 50s rock and roll music playing in the background. The place smelled of fried onions and grilled burgers, and I swear I could hear Ned's stomach growling as soon as we stepped in through the front door. We ordered cheeseburgers, fries and chocolate malts, and wolfed it all down in a matter of minutes. A more memorable meal I couldn't recall.

In fact, the entire day had been memorable, but after dinner it was time for us to make the long drive back to Minneapolis. As we pulled out of town, headlights cutting a path through the deep darkness, Ned turned to me and asked, "Dad, how come you don't come back here more often?"

I thought for a minute before answering, "Honestly? I don't know. I guess I've just moved on with my life. You know, with your mom and you and your sister and my job, I guess I've never felt I had the time."

He was silent for a minute before saying, "I liked it. It was fun being here."

"What'd you like most?" I asked, curious.

"Well…" After thinking about it for longer than I would have expected, he said, "I guess that it was just so different from where we live. But, different in a good way," he added, grinning. "It's not as crowded. The people were friendly. I liked Frisky." He paused, then said, "I don't know. It's hard to put into words."

I laughed. "Yeah, I get that."

He looked out the window for a moment, then turned and asked, "Dad, I was wondering… maybe we could come back again sometime. Would that be okay?"

I didn't have to think. The best part of the whole trip was sharing it with my son. "Sure," I told him. "Anytime."

He grinned. "Cool."

It wasn't exactly like it used to be, us talking together like we used to, not by a long shot. It was better.

Then we settled in for the long ride home, chatting back and forth, already planning for our next trip. I'm not saying a town can bring a father and son closer together, but, then again, who knows? Maybe it can. Especially if it's a town like Nativity.

About the author

Jim lives in a small town twenty miles west of Minneapolis, Minnesota. His stories have appeared online in *CafeLit*, *The Writers' Cafe Magazine*, *Cabinet of Heed*, *Paragraph Planet*, *Nailpolish Stories*, *Ariel Chart*, *Potato Soup Journal*, *Literary Yard*, *Spillwords* and *The Drabble*, and in print publications: *A Million Ways*, *Mused Literary Journal*, *Gleam Flash Fiction Anthology #2* and *The Best of CafeLit 8*. You can also check out his blog to see more:
www.theviewfromlonglake.wordpress.com.

The Unknown Path

Doug King

"It's been a long hard struggle, but finally we've got there," Billy Alsop announced with a huge sigh, stretching his long legs across the small study he was allocated at the university where he was a Fellow.

"What do you mean, a struggle?" his close friend Henry Worthing asked with a puzzled frown. "You've been sitting here all summer playing with that thing on your desk" pointing at the laptop computer. "No going out like we used to, no popping down to the local for a pint of real ale. In fact, no nothing. That is the sum total of your activities for weeks. I'm surprised your girlfriend puts up with it. I don't think I would, if I were her."

"Well, some things seem to be particularly important and these tend to take a little time. You know that, for a long while now, I have been debating and researching this idea about where we all come from: humans, life itself actually and, more particularly, where we may be going. So, I thought I would try and do something about it, hence I have applied my tiny mind and come up with a form of computer game. Incidentally, you are right," he went on. "Helen didn't put up with it. She packed up and left several weeks ago, but now I have finished my project I am going to persuade her to come back and try this game for herself."

"I thought I hadn't seen her about. It's a pity. I thought you and she were well suited. Not that I blame her, given the way you have been working. That is if you can call it working!"

"Oh, I can and I do. I have been working really hard." Billy leaned back in his chair and smiled at his friend. "You may not call it work, but then when it comes to computers you are a bit of a moron." He held up his hands in a gesture of submission when he saw Henry open his mouth to protest. "OK, I am being a bit harsh, you have many more skills with computer hardware than I have and you are a good programmer, but generally you use a computer to sort out problems in metal and suchlike and to write a few letters. I use a computer to create exciting new worlds. That's the difference between us."

"Is that what you have been doing? Or, are you kidding me again? Creating new worlds sounds a bit epic, even for you. What have you really been up to?"

His friend grinned broadly. "Playing games, of course. Well, writing one actually, and doing all the graphics as well. That's what I do best, that and thinking about life, the world and the universe."

"What's the universe got to do with it?" Henry demanded, actually sounding quite aggressive.

The two men had a rewarding friendship on many levels, but particularly when, as occurred regularly, they were discussing the pros and cons of an issue. They could be guaranteed to take opposing views on virtually any subject except politics. This was the one subject which they tacitly agreed not to discuss in anything but the most general terms. They followed the classic intellectual adage – if you can argue effectively against a subject or proposition then you can argue the case for the topic that much better. Friends and associates suspected that, if their agreed strictures where removed, then their opinions would have been remarkably similar.

Henry settled himself in a high-backed chair opposite his friend and crossed his legs. "Right then, tell me all about it. I know you've been quite secretive for some months and I suspect that the powerful computer I helped you build earlier in the year was part of this project of yours. Am I right?"

His friend nodded. "I have also been buying up bits and pieces such as the top-of-the-range Virtual Reality headsets and other add-ons for some time and making modifications to them as well. Meanwhile, I've been trying to write a program that will invite the participant to take part in and experience what I believe will be the next generation of computers."

"Interesting, and how does this thing work?"

"Oh, the working is simple. All you have to do is put on the VR headset and switch on the computer" Billy replied, with a silly grin on his face.

"Don't be so damned obtuse, you know exactly what I'm asking."

"My concept is, as we have previously discussed, that before too long man and computer will take on a joint existence; the one will support the other in many facets of our life. Homo sapiens, as the major dominant species in the world, will begin to morph into a technology-loaded creature."

"I still think that's a bit heavy." Henry shook his head. "Will that apply to, just the elite or will everyone be eligible for digital enhancement, because that's what you're talking about?"

"That is not a question I am in a position to answer." Billy paused. "That said I could probably do it now, if you really pushed me. However, think about where we've come from in the last sixty years. We have much more computer capacity in the mobile phone each of us carries around than there was for the first lunar landing. Then, when computers became bigger and more powerful Game Studios started writing games, mostly in the genre of what I call 'Thud and Blunder' computer games, where ridiculously over-developed, brain-dead heroes and some seriously sexy heroines, dressed in boob-armour and very little else, walk through hails of bullets and other junk to kill opponents and blow up buildings with huge guns."

Henry nodded in understanding and waited silently for his friend to continue.

Billy grinned. "But as we know that is games, dream merchant stuff, whereas in reality ordinary people are having pacemakers fitted, broken backs are being bypassed so people can walk again, and now there are brain implants as well."

"Yes, I can go along with that. Those things you have listed have been significant medical breakthroughs. Surely these innovations can only benefit mankind. But, I have a feeling that you are about to denounce such things. Why? I wonder."

"Wait." Billy held up his hand in a 'Stop' signal. "Surely you realise that this is only the very beginning? At the rate which technology is developing, even that of which we are aware, then the prophecies of the science fiction writers of the past half century and beyond will soon become true. That is, technology will soon be taking over from humans. It is a straightforward mathematical progression. We have Artificial Intelligence which can beat the greatest chess grand masters, AI can drive a car in crowded cities, fly and land a plane and do myriad other complex tasks. All AI really lacks, at the moment, is reasoning ability. I wonder if AI unaided by man will ever really understand the true meaning of the consequences of any action which is initiated by its computer. You know, in the same way that any intelligent human being would anticipate and understand the outcome of their actions in any given situation?"

"I take your point. To put it simply, will a computer

ever learn not to put its metaphorical finger in the fire. Yes, the argument is valid as far as it goes, but surely we scientists and mathematicians will always be able to control Artificial Intelligence and always insert limits and guidelines to restrict any possible excesses?" Henry scratched his head, a sure sign the he was beginning to worry about the future that Billy was describing.

There was silence between them for some moments while both contemplated the scenario, then Henry went on, "In an ideal world then the answer would be an unequivocal 'Yes'. We most certainly could and we should seek to limit the potential of every computer."

"But we don't live in an ideal world, do we? The question is 'Are we ever likely to'; I think not." Billy answered his own question. "We live in a world where parents cannot control the actions of their own children. There is no way that we can inhibit the programming skills of some young people with the knowledge to carry out advanced programming, but without either the wisdom or experience to be able to predict and understand the outcome."

"I can think of another problem," Henry leaned forward, interrupting his friend. "If, as seems likely, life did originate by accident in some primordial soup somewhere on this planet, many billions of years ago, what is there to stop another accident occurring whereby computers actually begin to reason and then create all on their own?"

Billy nodded, took a deep breath and then continued, "My dear friend, as both a scientist and as a human being this subject has concerned me. I have worried about this very thing for some time. Then I began to realise that as things stand, the one cannot exist without the other: humans and computers. We cannot go back and uninvent what is already is in existence, therefore we must, as a species go

191

forward and adapt to what we have created. In evolutionary terms it was nanoseconds ago that the first computer was invented and the chip was discovered and made viable. Such a very short time and we have come so far."

Henry stood up and began walking around the room, clearly very agitated by what Billy was describing to him. "There is another problem" he began. "Suppose it does happen, this integration of the human and the computer. Then what about all those people – the greater part of the human race – who will never benefit from all this new technology? Will it only be the exceptional individual and the cognoscenti who will ever be 'enhanced'? Won't the members of the general public be left in ignorance of what is actually happening?" He was again raising the question he had asked earlier in the discussion. "What will happen to them?"

"My guess is that they will have to manage with the technology they have here and now, mobile phones, Bluetooth, television and the like and that is all," Billy answered. "And that does concern me. I strongly suspect that powerful Artificial Intelligence, molecular engineering and cybernetics will become part and parcel of the future being incorporated into the bodies of the few, just as you have suggested. The controllers of the world, the chosen, will be the haves, while the have-nots will have nothing more than they have today. I seriously question whether that is ethical."

Henry paused in his perambulating and looked at his friend who was still reclining comfortably in his chair. "Yes, and what about infectious diseases and cancer. Will we still be attacking all those killer diseases and trying to relieve suffering for all the so called 'have-nots'?"

"Look, instead of us discussing these topics, which we have done many times before, why not find out what I think for yourself? All these issues and how I think it will all work out are set out in the game. Come and play the game or program, whatever you choose to call it. This will take you into the new world as I see it. It poses some questions and tries to answer others. Would you like to take part? I honestly believe that we, the likes of you and I, must be prepared to battle most of the current big players in the market. Already the big players are demanding that we comply with their need for voice recognition systems, our fingerprints and reading our irises, and this is going to go further. The proclaimed reason is better security for our devices, but in reality we have no privacy. These conglomerates know where we are, what we buy and when. Not to mention the many people who are giving even more private information away on all these social media websites."

"Yes, I really would like to see what you have done. It sounds very interesting. I will reserve all my questions and comments for afterwards, then I may have more questions. I may even have challenges for you."

"Good, I expect you will. I know I programmed the package, but I must tell you that I have been through the whole experience that you are about to have. Believe me, it will change your life." Billy rose from his chair to collect together all the equipment he needed if Henry was to fully experience the challenges that he had posed.

The most important piece of equipment was the Virtual Reality headset which fitted well over Henry's head and shoulders, and was carefully adjusted by Billy for an optimal fit. The controls were fixed to Henry's wrists and fingers before he was allowed to settle into a deep chair and wait for his friend to initiate the program.

Once Henry was settled, Billy moved over to his laptop that was hooked up to an exceedingly powerful static computer that Henry had helped build. He initiated the program and sat back to watch his friend. At one point, Henry tried to touch the back of his neck, which was covered by the VR helmet, but apart from that he was completely enthralled.

Once the program had ended Billy removed the heavy helmet. Henry rubbed the back of his neck, just above the hairline and turned to Billy. The two men looked at each other and smiled. "That is an amazing program with some terrifying conclusions."

The two had been friends since school days. Doctor William Charles David Alsop was a person of exceptional intelligence who had dedicated his academic career to trying to find the origins of life on earth and, by examining the past, to attempt to project in to the future what life might become. His friend Doctor Henry George Worthing, who was equally intelligent, but with different gifts, had been retained by a number of aircraft manufacturers across the globe to examine issues of metal fatigue and excessive wear in components. His hobby was restoring old cars, while his friend, Billy, was absorbed by the potential of computers.

"I thought something was stuck in my neck, at the base of my skull at one point but everything feels OK." Henry paused for a moment. "Do you mind if I think this whole experience through before I comment further?" He looked up at the wall clock. "Just, look at the time. I promised to meet a couple of my students at the pub for a quick drink and a review of their recent research."

However, the computer thought otherwise and he found himself settling into the worn armchair. Once he was seated he heard a voice in his head, a voice with which, in the future, he would become very familiar, "Welcome to your Nativity, Henry."

About the author

In the past I have had a few articles published, mainly relating to Psychology and Personal Development. My writing expertise is really in the field of technical writing. This is my first attempt at a short story and I was put up to it by my friend/partner who is much better at this, so blame her.

Tick Tock

Sally Angell

No – o – o – oh!

The door of side Room 4 burst open and a woman, still doing her clothes up, charged out across the waiting area to Reception.

"Call this a service?" She banged on the desk, wiping her nose on a dangling sleeve. "I want to make a complaint!"

How awful. No rings, Joy could see from where she was sitting. And it was *Ms* Anderson. The name had flashed on the screen, for the 3.30pm slot. So single most likely and from the state of her, going private wasn't an option. Joy shuddered. Think of it. The end of a dream. What must that feel like? But (guilty pang), it meant another place available, for someone else.

We're all desperate for a referral.

Tick tock. How much longer? Joy lifted the arm next to her to check the time: 3.45pm. Alan always wore a watch. He liked retro stuff, and it was comforting, indicating long-term values in a throw-away world. Alan himself was staring at the pictures on the walls, strumming his fingers on the iPaper he'd bought from the newsstand. He had that look. *What am I doing here?*

He wasn't the only one. The other would-be parents squirmed on the clinic's chrome and black chairs, not looking at each other. They'd all heard. A few minutes ago, in some bizarre button/tannoy mix up, the smooth professional tones had boomed into their midst, from inside the consulting room.

"You don't meet the criteria, madam!" Words that they all dreaded having to hear.

The shock of that, and the scene afterwards had been

unsettling. And now the distressed woman had cornered a nurse, pinning her to the wall to make her 'b----y listen' to how she'd been treated.

A tall man and his partner were arguing. He stood up, she pushed him down, and they left, pushing each other, her shouting, "You'd make a terrible father anyway."

Alan laughed and went red. Joy sighed. Who was left then? A lady in a headscarf, sitting apart from the others, closed her eyes. There was one more couple, though they were probably seeing the other consultant. Plus herself and Alan.

3.57pm. With a nervous tummy, Joy eyed the screen. She was next. The latest bullet points for acceptance for treatment, which she had googled, were printed on her brain.

1) A long-term marriage
2) Repeated attempts to conceive naturally
3) A medical problem

The stakes were so high. Joy longed for it all to be over, for this excruciating anxiety to stop. But if the answer was No, how could she bear it. The *neverness.* To never know what motherhood was like, never assuage the longing.

Ms Anderson, ignored by the staff, was still hovering. It was her eyes that chilled Joy; opaque and still. No-one behind them.

crackle…

Joy froze. Oh, not again.

"These ladies!" It was the same voice, the voice of God-man, the revered one, who held their futures, and children, in his hands. Only it didn't sound like him.

"It's about them. Their lives. Their careers. Then, when *they* want to play mummy, I, Sanjay, must perform the miracles." Mutterings… money and resources.

Everyone knew budgets had been slashed. But oh, the betrayal. Where had polite, understanding Doctor Sharma gone? Her eyes swivelled over to the Happy Family wall-posters. And the slogan:

IT'S *YOUR* RIGHT TO HAVE *YOUR* CHILD

Well, not for the last patient, who was blundering over to the exit. Her skirt, already skewed, had got caught up at the back, and she misjudged the doorway, banging into the glass pane.

4pm: the digits shone up from Joy's mobile. "Mrs Farook to Room 5," the girl called. The electronic screen had gone blank. "Mr and Mrs Williams – that way."

This was it, then. Joy forced breath in… one, two three and out four, five, six. Ha! Theirs was the last appointment of the day, before his lordship went on annual leave. His head would already be up in the clouds, she'd reasoned, half-way to the sunshine villa. They, she and Alan, had this one chance to have what most people had without thinking. Someone of their own, that they had created, to love.

Her body rose and followed the footsteps of the receptionist. Somewhere in her head, she was aware of Alan, all sweaty beside her.

"Let me do the talking," she heard herself say. Alan's mouth opened in confusion. He'd spent weeks rehearsing his lines. But she daren't risk it. Not with these odds.

It was *Mr* Sharma, not Doctor, due to his high status, Joy reminded herself as they went in. So she addressed him correctly, and made herself shake hands and smile a fake smile. Time to go for it. No one was going to give a damn if they didn't meet the criteria. This man, and the nameless authorities who made the decisions, held the supreme power to create a new life, or not. What gave them the right?

And Joy knew. *She* must make it happen, take any risk. Now.

"So." He was reading the online questionnaire Joy's GP had filled in with her, and emailed him. "You've been married for…"

"Nine years." Joy smiled dreamily at Alan, fingering the ring she'd found at a recent antiques market. Her breath stuck in her throat. Hospital departments didn't hold computerized personal or medical patient details. When a friend had an op recently, she was given a paper form listing illnesses to put a cross by if she'd had them.

So all the consultant actually had was the email, and notes from a general information chat last month. Joy's GP was new, hadn't got full access to notes yet, and had accepted her answers. No one would have time to check. But talk about treading through a live minefield.

"Right." Mr Sharma was nodding, so fingers crossed. Mr Williams' swimmers were within the required range… Thumbs up to Alan.

"So, the problem is with you, Mrs Williams, as we suspected. Ah… you've had the examination at your local Outpatients – good." Blah de blah, technical stuff.

The inner clicking started up, like tinnitus, in Joy's skull. Ticktocktick tockticktock. This could be it, the deadline, the last half hour, last five minutes even of her creative span. Her body locked in paralysis, alert for the alarm set by an unknown hand to start jangling. *Too late.*

He spun his chair round to face them.

It hadn't been so much a lightbulb moment. More, it seemed to Joy, of an accumulation of flashes. After whole chunks of her twenties and early thirties spent with men who turned out to be Mr Wrong/Commitment Phobe/Shitbag, she got the picture.

"I'm not going to find Mr Right."

"It's your generation," everyone said. Altered lifestyles. The changing roles of women. But it was also, Joy could see, how girls were fed Fairy Tales, no matter when they were born. Stories that happened in a timeless space or could cover centuries of old beliefs, they promised an idealized love and happy ending.

If only she could rewind her lifetime so far, make the mechanism go anti-clockwise, while knowing what she knew now. And do things differently. But she could only go forward and try to sort the mess out.

All the options were daunting. She had friends who'd gone online for a donor. A bit dodgy, in Joy's book. Unknown. Anon. He could be a murderer. Or have some other undesirable physical or genetic flaw. And how would she explain it to a son or daughter in the future? They might hate her, after all. No, she decided. Not unless I have to.

"How would you feel," she broached the subject to Alan, while they were watching the Nordic thriller on TV, "about being a daddy?" Well, no use pussyfooting around. They'd been friends for years.

"I'm not married," Alan grinned quirkily. "Oh you mean—"

They could have a child together, she said. People did.

A well-known actress had done it. She'd given an interview in the Sunday paper. Her male BF had been standing by the washing-machine, she'd looked at him, and had seduced him by the end of the spin cycle.

"But I'd be an OAP, an official old git – before it left school." Alan took a huge swig of lager.

"So? What about all these geriatric rockstars, going on fathering into their seventies."

There was that, Alan agreed. And he'd always wanted children.

"But having a kid – shouldn't we be in love?"

She flinched. Funny how that hurt.

"No. What I mean is – I've always fancied you, liked you. It's just – families these days, how everything is."

"I know." Joy nodded. "It would have to be IVF," she added. "My plumbing."

There was the faintest disappointment in his eyes. And hers too, as they looked at each other in the way people did when vaguely considering whether an intimate relationship was a possibility.

They needn't live together, needn't co-habit, Joy explained. Well (private aside), perhaps he could stay over when nights descended into a crying fest. And help with the baby too!

But having someone *there*, all the time, when she wanted to slop around in a stained fleece, not have to speak, or pretend to be normal? It was the conundrum of living in an age of anxiety; wanting a relationship but not being able to cope with the reality of one.

Alan said he would think about it.

In the euphoria of a Yes to their fertilization treatment, Joy thought she could wish for no more. Somewhere on her lifeline, this was meant to be. Two fingers up, then, to the writing-off of wombs.

But it was only the first lap of the marathon, the first obstacle knocked down. Long days at the Treatment Centre were draining. Apart from the injections, all the prodding and poking, every inch of her hurt.

"Hello!"

Joy, there for the fourth time that week, looked up. She hated that, when someone obviously knew her but she hadn't the foggiest who they were. Just have to blag it, and hope they gave a clue. Yet there was something…

"Elizabeth – from the referral centre."

Oh – my – gosh!

"I appealed on grounds of ageist and female discrimination. Got an awesome compensation package."

It was her. Ms Anderson. Close up, the lines were deeper, the hair thinner, the chin more jowly than under the eco lighting in the clinic. But happiness shone over all that, giving her a glow of youth.

Birmingham?

The admissions officer nodded. Mrs Williams would have to go there for the birth, because of her medical condition, so they'd book her in for her due date.

"But we live in Bedfordshire." Alan did the mental geographics.

There is a link the officer announced proudly, between this hospital and the Birmingham Specialist Centre. Joy's brain pinged. She was getting expert at spotting these glib one-liners. Unreality check.

When they'd got the news that the embryo had taken, nothing else had seemed to matter. Sometimes, in the morning, her body would stir to a hug of softness against her body, that smell, so *real*. Like when you dreamed of something *so* good and in that dream you pleaded. Please don't let me wake up.

She'd started working from home, the days melding into each other so she was hardly aware of the hour, or the moment. Just the presence inside. And being.

But the hospital circus continued. How stupid, Joy sighed tiredly, travelling to a city miles away in a month when everything, especially vulnerable people, started dying. How could she self-care, support the life inside her, give it the best chance of survival, when the system was so idiotic?

It would be November, she said sharply. They'd have to use public transport. "My husband doesn't drive. And it'll be winter."

"We can't change the weather, Miss."

Joy bit down so hard, her teeth crunched. No. She meant she'd need to go in the night before. And anyway they couldn't know for sure *when* it would happen. Her head throbbed, at this strange disinterest in the patient's well-being.

They didn't do admissions the night before.

There was no reservation the Travelodge said, for anyone named Williams. Joy said her husband had pre-booked it on his tablet in August. She had to have somewhere to stay tonight. She was so tired.

There was a room, a single. She'd have to wait, they said, while they cleared it up. So she sat in the lobby in an Ikea chair, hands cradling the taut sore sphere of her stomach. Someone gave her a blanket. The lad on the desk brought her tea. And a child nearby put a jelly baby in her hand.

The last few hours had been a jumble of pain and confusion, of whispering "It's just me and you, you and me," to the rhythm of the train. She remembered standing on the platform to get the 3pm on Midlands Mainline, and the red light bobbing in the text box on her mobile. He was in A & E, Alan's message read. *My knee's gone. Just follow the instructions on the timetable printout. A. I mean, Love Alan.*

So much for a partner. Joy's *Woman Today* magazine advised treating men as entertainment, not relying on them to help in emergencies. But there was still that little girl in Joy, who trusted daddy to keep her safe, to make everything all right.

The room was ready. It was cold and smelled funny.

The only furniture was a single bed. There was no light in the bathroom. But the shower was hot, flowing over the contours of her body like a warm waterfall, flowing, flowing into her, flowing waters, flowing water, flowing out from her, flowing... waters.

"Oh Mum! Help me." She took two Nurofen, and two more. Light-headed, she phoned a taxi from the list on the wall. Then she was outside in her coat, waiting, waiting for the taxi, paper towels dripping onto her bag. Not long now. Not long now.

Blazing lights lit up the clock on the outside of the Specialist Centre building. They must be doing renovations. The bronze and silver clock had no hands, no numbers. Just a blank face.

Everything was slowing down, but in a good way. Down to the delivery room, a white-gold light above. Her head expanded – eons of history squee-e-e-z-ed into Now.

Something's wrong. Joy can't hear anything, not the skip of a clock hand not a breath. Nothing.

silence
suspension
stopped

1.am:
A cry.
Restart. The beginning.

About the author
Sally Angell loves literature and writing, and is always aiming to develop new and original ideas in her work. Sally explores the truth and reality of feelings, the originality of language and the possibilities of words. She likes to write stories with contemporary themes, that also have a universal meaning. Her writing has been published in magazines and anthologies, and read on radio.

What Goes Around

Allison Symes

"Sorry, Annie, but that's how it is and in these days of cost cutting, something has to give."

"Are you enjoying driving your brand new BMW, Mr Smythe?"

Annie enjoyed seeing her boss blush. *It's nice to be wrong, I didn't think the slimy old toad could do that.*

"It's a vital part of our corporate image, Annie..."

"And having a clean, comfortable environment to work in isn't? Customers often comment on that."

"Yes, but we have other cleaners, Annie, and you have been forgetting things and coming in late every day for the last month. You've given no reasons why."

It was Annie's turn to blush. *How can I explain my house guest, who turned up out of nowhere, is causing chaos and I can't get rid of her? Why did Rosie pick me? She promised to turn my life around. Said I would have a new beginning and no more rotten luck. Ha! I was an idiot falling for that. But the promise of a new life has fooled many over time, not just Muggins here.*

"I'll miss working here, Mr Smythe. I'll get my coat." *There's no way I am explaining Rosie, even if I could.*

"I've got the sack, Rosie, that's why I'm home early, and it is your fault. You said you would bring blessings to me and my home if I could shelter you for a while. You've brought nothing but chaos. Tell me again, why did you *really* get expelled from your world?"

Rosie scowled. "I got the push because they said I'm too old to perform magic anymore. My spells keep going wrong."

205

Annie looked up at the scorch marks on her ceiling. "I'll say."

"I am sorry, Annie. I will make it up to you. I was serious about having a new start in life and, given you need one too after all you've been through, it makes sense for us to help each other. My trouble is I think the magic goes wrong when I'm stressed. Tell you what, and as you believed my story…"

"And cleared up your messes…"

"Yes, that too. As I was saying, you can have three wishes. I don't dole those out to just anyone."

"You've got to be kidding me. I spent all of last night clearing up the bathroom. That water and soap went everywhere. As for the kitchen, you're not going near the cooker again. I didn't know what to say to the service guy when he came out. There is no logical explanation to finding a magic wand stuck in my old Rayburn. You know I treasure that. Dear Mum left it to me with this place and…"

"I said I'm sorry. What more can I say or do?"

"Just don't do magic again. We'll all have a peaceful life then. You did say you wanted a new start, a new type of life, so go for that option and you'll help me out too."

"The Fairy Queen also said I should forget magic and that it was a pity it hadn't forgotten me," Rosie sniffed loudly, picked up her now cold cup of tea and slurped it down in one big noisy go.

Annie winced. Had Rosie been given the push from her old world for her lack of etiquette, Annie wouldn't have been surprised. Nor did she feel inclined to encourage Rosie to feel sorry for herself. Rosie was pretty good at that as it was.

"I'm looking for another cleaning job from tomorrow. Please don't interfere. If you want to help me, do some gardening for me without magic. I've got autumn flowering bulbs to put in the D-shaped border. Give it a go. Follow the packet instructions and plant them manually. It can be therapeutic getting your hands dirty. And I love it when the flowers come to life later on. Cheers me up as the evenings draw in so early."

Rosie looked at her tiny perfect hands. "Can't I...?"

"Not one bit of magic, I mean it, Rosie. If it makes you feel better, treat this as a wish from me."

Rosie smiled. "It does, Annie, it so does. And I can't go wrong with granting this wish either!"

Annie made herself smile. *I hope you're right, Rosie, else my garden will look like a war zone by the time you've finished with it, but I've got to get you doing something remotely useful to stop you finding your own entertainment. If you do drop the magic, we will all be better off for it! The sooner you realise that, the better. The sooner you'll move on and be happier for it too.*

A new chance in life doesn't mean doing the same thing over and over again until you get it right. You could wait decades for that to happen... I haven't got decades left. Not sure my nerves would stand it even if I did. The house certainly won't!

"Annie, can't I do one teeny weeny spell on the weather? It's rained heavily for a fortnight and you've gone and got another job in that time."

Annie frowned. *It was great the hospital job came up, it's the perfect new start for me, it's lovely, so are the people there, and Rosie swears she had nothing to do with it. A job comes up so fast and I get it just like that. Told I'm the very person they've been looking for. Heard good things about me. From where? I wonder!*

"Rosie, absolutely not. The weather is God's department.

Don't meddle. The forecast is better tomorrow and the soil will be nice and soft after all the rain."

Annie picked up her chocolate chip shortbread and took a huge bite out of it. Rosie had already scoffed three. The shortbread had been in the house for ten minutes. At least magic wasn't involved there. Shortbread was shortbread and a rare treat for Annie but now some money was coming in again, the odd indulgence was good for the soul, though possibly not the waistline. Still nobody ever had it all. And Annie had shortbread.

"I really want to get those bulbs in for you, Annie. I've been looking forward to it. I like being in the garden. I liked your story to the neighbours I'm a distant cousin with a height deficiency! That was quick thinking," Rosie laughed. The tinkling sound made Annie's tea cup rattle.

Annie smiled. "You can garden tomorrow."

Annie was late home the next day and wasn't surprised, as she walked down the drive, to see Rosie peering out of the lounge window. Annie's childhood border collie, Mabel, often did the same when she knew Annie was due home, and, strangely, Rosie had exactly the same expression on her face as the dog once did. That combination of hope, excitement and can't get to the door quickly enough to greet you kind of look.

Annie's heart raced. If Rosie had something to tell her, it was likely to be bad news, but Annie was pleased to be wrong. Her garden *was* still there after Rosie's handiwork *and* the D-shaped border was full of beautiful crocuses in rainbow colours. "Rosie, the flowers are meant to come up in the autumn, not immediately! Whatever will the neighbours think… No flower grows that fast."

"I told them I had special fertilizer not available in the shops. They think it's something off the internet, so don't worry. It *is* amazing what you *can* get off the web, are you sure there's no magic involved here somewhere? No? Anyway, I said I'd get the neighbours some of the special fertilizer when it's next available but couldn't say when. They were happy with that. Is that all right?"

Annie nodded. "Well done. Nice bit of quick thinking from you there! It's just a shame I'll have no crocuses to look forward to later, that's all."

"You will, Annie. I used up a wish for you. This lot will keep blooming till November. The bees will love that too. Why are you late? You should have been back two hours, five minutes and forty seconds ago."

Annie smiled. "Timing me, were you? I was just finishing my stint when I saw my old boss, Mr Smythe, come in. I went and said hello and we got chatting. He seemed pleased to see me. Said it was nice to see a friendly face again. Oh and if I wanted my old job back, he'd arrange it. Apparently I'm missed. It looks like I worked harder than the others. It is so nice to know that! Would you believe it but he's only gone and crashed his shiny new car right into that wall near Tesco? He's okay but annoyed as his bosses won't replace it and he wrote the thing off apparently."

"So much for his corporate image then, Annie!"

Annie stared at the innocent looking Rosie. "I didn't tell you that, Rosie. You must've been eavesdropping somehow. All I said was I'd been fired and…"

"It was my fault. I said I'd make it up to you, Annie. If there's something every decent magical being wants, it's a happy ending for those who are kind to us, Annie. I delivered, Annie, I delivered! This is the new start for my magic I wanted. Look out, world! This fairy is *back* and on top of her game again."

Annie sighed. And the day had gone so well too. Maybe new beginnings would have to wait for another time after all.

About the author

Allison Symes is published by Chapeltown Books, Cafe Lit, and Bridge House Publishing amongst others. She is a member of the Society of Authors and Association of Christian Writers. Her website is www.allisonsymescollectedworks.wordpress.com and she blogs for Chandler's Ford Today: http://chandlersfordtoday.co.uk/author/allison-symes/.

Index of Authors

Sally Angell, 196
Jim Bates, 180
Margaret Bulleyment, 65
Finn Clarke, 136
Elizabeth Cox, 108
Jeanne Davies, 52
Alyson Faye, 129
Nicole Fitton, 116
Linda Flynn, 104
I L Green, 156
Vanessa Horn, 28
Janet Howson, 140
Doug King, 187
Dawn Knox, 92
Joy Mawby, 176
Maeve Murphy, 33
Aqsa Mustafa, 120
Adrian Naylor, 8
Paula R C Readman, 144
L F Roth, 83
Nicolas Siregar, 166
Dianne Stadhams, 21
Allison Symes, 205
Steve Wade, 57

Other Publications by Bridge House

Crackers

edited by Debz Hobbs-Wyatt and Gill James

Every year we pick a very vaguely Christmas-related theme for our annual anthology. Then we invite our writers to subvert it. In this collection, they've certainly done that to the extent that we almost had a picture of cream crackers for the cover. Our theme this year is "crackers". So, we have Christmas crackers, cream crackers, cracking dresses, a cracked antique and many, many other interpretations. We hope you will find this a cracking good read.

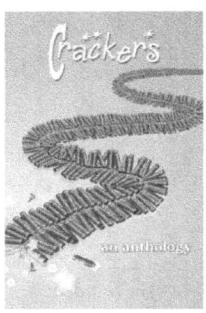

"A wonderfully quirky and eccentric collection of short stories. Each one has a different take on the notion of 'crackers' with a heart of darkness resonating throughout. A book of little morality gems!" (*Amazon*)

Order from www.bridgehousepublishing.co.uk

Paperback: ISBN 978-1-907335-59-4
eBook: ISBN 978-1-907335-60-0

Glit-er-ary

edited by Debz Hobbs-Wyatt and Gill James

This glittery collection of glit-er-ary tales will add some
sparkle to your life. You will meet all kinds of interesting
characters facing all kinds of interesting dilemmas.

You will learn that all that glitters is most certainly not gold.
The stories are funny, sad, poignant… the glitter comes in
shades of dark and light. But all will leave their sparkle in
your imagination.

"This book is a little gem. Some beautiful writing - thoroughly
enjoyed this as something to dip in and out of for some much
needed escapism" (*Amazon*)

Order from www.bridgehousepublishing.co.uk

Paperback: ISBN 978-1-907335-55-6
eBook: ISBN 978-1-907335-56-3

Baubles

edited by Debz Hobbs-Wyatt and Gill James

The challenge was to write a bauble of a story. So we have a varied selection of snippets that sparkle. Once again we feel privileged to publish this fine group of writers. Each story is different and glitters in its own way.

"A great range of stories and styles here. A story for everyone. Talented, contemporary writers writing about issues that engage you." (*Amazon*)

Order from www.bridgehousepublishing.co.uk

Paperback: ISBN 978-1-907335-46-4
eBook: ISBN 978-1-907335-47-1

www.ingramcontent.com/pod-product-compliance
Lightning Source LLC
Chambersburg PA
CBHW061151170626
46809CB00003B/1052